THE
SICILIAN BOSS'S
MISTRESS

THE
SICILIAN BOSS'S
MISTRESS

BY

PENNY JORDAN

First published in Great Britain 2009
Large Print edition 2009
Harlequin Mills & Boon Limited,
Eton House, 18-24 Paradise Road,
Richmond, Surrey TW9 1SR

© Penny Jordan 2009

ISBN: 978 0 263 20618 0

Set in Times Roman 16½ on 19¾ pt.
16-0909-51619

Harlequin Mills & Boon policy is to use papers that are
natural, renewable and recyclable products and made
from wood grown in sustainable forests. The logging and
manufacturing process conform to the legal environmental
regulations of the country of origin.

Printed and bound in Great Britain
by CPI Antony Rowe, Chippenham, Wiltshire

CHAPTER ONE

THE bed on which they both lay naked was high, draped with richly sensuous silk fabric. But its touch against her flesh was nowhere near as sensuously erotic as *his* touch, nor could the whisper of the fabric's kiss compare with the fierce passion of *his* kiss.

His face was in the shadows, but she knew its features by heart—from the burning intensity of his dark eyes through the arrogance of his profile to the explicit sensuality of his mouth. Excited pleasure curled and then kicked through her. Simply looking at him awoke and aroused the woman in her in a way and at a level that no other man ever could. Just as she was the only woman who was woman enough to truly complement him as a man. They were made for one another, a perfect match, and they both knew it. Only here, with him, could she truly be herself and let down her guard to share her longing and her love.

He made her ache for him in a thousand—no, a hundred thousand different ways, and the way his knowing smile lifted the corners of his mouth told her that he *knew* that her whole body shuddered in mute delight at the slow, deliberate stroke of his fingertips along the curve of her breast.

She sucked in her breath and closed her eyes. His stroking hand moved lower, over her quivering belly, and then lower…

Guiltily Leonora shook herself out of her daydream and warned herself that if she didn't start getting ready and stop wasting time she was going to be late.

What a fool she was. Her brothers would certainly think so. She could just imagine the hoots of derision with which they would have greeted her fantasy—and the secret of her own deeply sensual nature.

That was the trouble with growing up a girl sandwiched in the middle of two brothers. The three of them had been born so close together that Piers was only eighteen months older than her, and Leo a year younger. The fact that they had lost their mother so early, killed by a speeding driver as she was on her way to meet them from junior school, had naturally affected them all—including their father, an ex-professional sportsman who had retired from his sport to manage and then take over a sportswear manufacturing company. Their father had believed in fostering competition between his children as a way of preparing them for the adult world. He was also very much a stiff-upper-lip kind of man. After their mother's death Leonora had felt she had to work even harder at being 'one of the boys' for her father's sake, so that she wouldn't let the side down by crying like a girl.

Her father loved them all very much, but he was an old-fashioned man's man, and he hadn't been very good at showing that love to a motherless daughter. Not that Leonora blamed him for anything. In fact she was fiercely defensive of both him and her brothers, and they were even as adults a close-knit family. But not so close knit that they hadn't welcomed their new stepmother when their father had remarried three years ago. But watching her father unbend and get in touch with his emotions under the gentle tutelage of his second wife had reinforced for Leonora how much she had lost with her mother.

It was only her pride that kept her going sometimes, as she struggled with her growing need to be the woman she instinctively knew she might have been against the often harsh reality of being the competitive tomboy girl her father had taught her to be. Sometimes she felt so helpless and lost that she was afraid that she would *never* find her real self. Sometimes when she was being true to her real self and one of her brothers laughed at her she felt so crushed that she retreated immediately into the combative sibling hostility of their childhood.

And sometimes, like now, she took refuge in private dreams.

The fact that she needed to fantasise about being with a man who loved and desired her, and with whom she could have wonderful sensual sex, instead of actually knowing what it felt like from first-hand experience was, of course, partly a result of the way she had grown up. Listening to her brothers discussing their own sexual experimentation had made her wary of being judged and found wanting, as they so often seemed to judge other girls.

Leonora didn't consider herself to be the cringing, over-sensitive type, but there was something about the way her brothers, as pubescent boys, had talked about girls—giving them scores for availability, looks and sexual skill—that had made her believe that she never, ever wanted to wonder if some boy was talking to his friends about her in the way that her brothers had about girls. Because of that she had fought against and denied the depth of her own passionate nature, concealing it instead with a jokey 'one of the boys' manner.

Whilst other girls had been learning to be confident with their sexuality on their way to becoming women, somehow she had learned to fear hers.

It was different now, of course. Her brothers had grown up and, at twenty-seven and twenty-four, were well past the teenage stage of discussing their sex lives and their girlfriends with anyone.

She had grown up too, and at twenty-five felt

uncomfortably self-conscious about her still-virginal state, and very thankful that no one, most especially her brothers, knew about it. Not that she allowed herself to think about her lack of sexual experience very often, other than in that self-protective jokey way she had developed. She had more important things to worry about, such as getting a job. Or rather getting *the* job, she admitted, as she stepped into the shower and turned on the water.

As children, all three of them had been skinny and tall. Whilst Piers and Leo had broadened out, Leonora—whilst not skinny—was still very slender for her five-feet-nine-inch height. But her skin was still golden from a late October holiday in the Canary Islands the previous year, and her breasts were softly rounded, with dark pert nipples, and just that bit too full for her to go braless. In her tomboy days she had longed to be able to do so, hating the unwanted restriction of 'girls' clothes' as she struggled to compete with her elder brother and at the same time make sure that her younger brother knew his place.

The life-long fate of the poor middle child, she

thought ruefully, and a struggle that was still ongoing now.

She was out of the shower as speedily as she had stepped into it, crossing her bedroom floor on long, slim legs and drying herself as she did so, her long dark hair a tangle of damp curls.

Her pilot's uniform lay on the bed, and her heart did a somersault as she looked at it. Leo had complained so much about the loss of his spare uniform over Christmas, when they had all gone home to Gloucestershire to spend Christmas, that she had felt sure that someone in the family would suspect her—especially as Leo had already promised to let her take his place. But luckily nothing had been said.

Poor Mavis, who worked at the dry cleaners two streets away from the tiny London flat Leonora rented, had protested that there was no way she could adjust the jacket to fit her, never mind the hat. But Leonora had told her that she had every faith in her, and ultimately that faith had been rewarded.

Leonora knew that many of her friends thought that she was very lucky to work freelance, giving private lessons in Mandarin, but it hadn't been with becoming a language coach in mind that Leonora had honed her gift for languages, adding Russian and Mandarin to her existing French and Italian.

Life just wasn't fair at times, and it seemed to treat a person even more unfairly when she was a girl with two brothers. *She* had been the one to say first that more than anything else she wanted to learn to fly and become an airline pilot, but it was her younger brother who was now on his way to having her dream job—piloting the privately owned jet of the billionaire owner of a private airline based near Florence—whilst she, with all her flying qualifications, was teaching Mandarin. But then, as her elder brother had commented on more than one occasion, it was her own fault for insisting on qualifying in a world in which it was always going to be difficult for a woman to make her mark.

There were women pilots, of course—any number of them, but a humdrum job flying in and out of one of Britain's regional airports wasn't what Leonora wanted. Nor was it what she had trained for. No—her aspirations went much higher than that.

As a middle child, and a girl sandwiched between two brothers, Leonora felt as though she'd had to fight all her life to make her voice heard and her presence felt. Well, today she was certainly going to be doing that, when she took her brother's place at the controls of the private jet belonging to the owner of Avanti Airlines.

Leo had tried to wriggle out of letting her do it, as she had known he would, but she had reminded him that he owed her a birthday present and a big, *big* favour for introducing him to Angelica, his stunningly beautiful Polish girlfriend.

'Be reasonable,' he had protested. 'I can't possibly let you take my place.'

But Leonora had no intention of being reasonable. *Reasonable* went with the kind of girls who were sexually self-assured, whom men adored and flirted with. Not someone like her, who had put up barriers around herself, acting the jokey tomboy, always ready for a dare. She had done it for so long that she didn't think she would ever be able to find her way back to the woman she might have been. Far easier now to simply carry on being outrageous, always ready to challenge either of her brothers—or indeed any man—at his own game and win, than to admit that sometimes she longed desperately to be a different kind of girl.

Alessandro had been frowning when he left the meeting he had come to London to attend, and he was still frowning twenty minutes later, when he got out of the limousine at the Carlton Tower Hotel, despite the fact that the meeting had gone very well.

A tall man, he carried himself with what other men often tended to think was arrogance but which women knew immediately was the confidence of a man who knew what it was to experience the true give and take of sensual pleasure. The facial features stamped onto the sun-warmed Sicilian flesh might have been those of a warrior Roman Emperor tempered by endurance into a fierce strength. They signalled that pride, and a sense of being set apart from or even above other men. His dark hair, with its strong curl, was close-cropped to his head, and the eyes set beneath dark brows and framed with thick dark lashes were an extraordinary shade of dark grey. When he moved there was a leanness about his movements, a hint of the hunter intent on the swift capture of its prey. Men treated him with wary respect. Women were intrigued by him and desired him.

The doorman recognised him and greeted him by name, and the pretty receptionist eyed him covertly as he strode through the foyer, busy with designer-clad women and their escorts, heading for the lift.

In his jacket pocket was the cause of his irritation—a formal invitation, and with it a letter that was more a command than a fraternal request, from his elder brother, reminding him that his presence would be expected at the weekend of celebrations to mark the nine-hundredth anniversary of the granting to his family of their titles. They were due to begin tomorrow evening, and were being held at the family's main residence on Sicily. His absence was not an option.

And of course whenever Falcon, the eldest of

the three of them, made such a statement it was the duty of his younger siblings to support him— just as he had always supported them during the years of their shared childhood when they had suffered so much.

On this occasion, though, Rocco, their younger brother, had been granted a leave of absence from his family duty as he was on honeymoon, and Alessandro had thought that *he* was going to get away with not going in view of the buy-out negotiations he was involved in with another airline. But Falcon's ironic sending of the formal invitation together with a letter of reminder made it plain that he expected Alessandro to be there.

He and Falcon would be the only two of their father's sons to attend, with Rocco away. Antonio, their younger half-brother, would not be there. He was dead, killed in a car accident, as a result of which their father, who had loved his youngest son with far more emotion and in-tensity than he had felt for his eldest three all put together, had developed a terminal heart condi-tion from which he was not expected to survive for more than a year at best.

Only his own brothers could know and understand why Alessandro felt so little sorrow at the
thought of his father's demise, since they had all
shared the same childhood. It was Antonio their
father had loved, not them. No one had loved
them. Not their mother, whose death after
Rocco's birth had meant that she had not been
there to love them, and certainly not their father.

Alessandro gazed towards the window, not
seeing the view of Carlton Gardens that lay
beyond it but seeing instead the dark shadows of
Castello Leopardi, and the room where he had
lain staring into the darkness after his father had
mocked him for crying for his dead mother.

'Only a fool and a weakling fool cries for a
woman. But then that is exactly what you are—
a worthless second son who will never be
anything other than second best. Remember that
when you are a man, Alessandro. All you will
ever be is second best.'

Second best. How those words had tortured and
haunted him. And how they had driven him as well.

But it had not been his first-born, Falcon,
whom their father had loved beyond reason. It

had been Antonio, the only child of their father's second marriage to a woman who had been his mistress for years, who had humiliated and shamed their own mother with their father's help. Antonio—sly, manipulative, well aware of the power he'd had over their father's affections and how to make use of it to his own best advantage—had not been liked by *any* of his three half-brothers, but Alessandro acknowledged that he'd probably had more reason to dislike him than either of his siblings.

He might have distanced himself now from the boy he had been—the child who had grown up being told by his father that his only role in life was to play second fiddle to his elder brother, a spare heir in case anything should happen to Falcon—but the scars from having grown up always feeling that he had to justify his existence and prove that he was of value were still there.

On the day of his seventh birthday party, after some childish quarrel with his half-brother during which Antonio had started mimicking their father, taunting him by telling him their father loved him the best, he had retaliated by saying that he was the second eldest.

Their father had told spoken to him coldly. 'You are a second son—conceived so that if necessary you can take your elder brother's place. You as yourself have and are nothing. A second son is of no account whilst there is a first-born. Think about that in future, when you attempt to place yourself above your youngest brother, for God knows I wish with all my heart that he might have been my only son.'

Strange the powerful effect that words could have. His father had meant to humiliate and shame him for daring to stand against the favouritism he showed to his youngest son; he had wanted to cow him and make him feel inferior. But his cruelty had had exactly the opposite effect, burning into Alessandro a determination to forge a life for himself that had no reliance on the Leopardi name or his father's influence.

Instead of becoming a part of the old feudal world of his father and family history, Alessandro had turned towards the new, modern world, where a man was judged on his business acumen and his personal achievements. He had adopted his mother's family name instead of using his own, and that name was still proudly displayed on the fleet of aircraft that had earned him his billionaire status—even though these days he was secure enough in what and who he was to answer to both Leopardi and Avanti.

He had proved beyond any kind of doubt that he had no need of his father's help or his father's name, and in fact it now amused him to see the frustrated lack of understanding in his father's expression when he adapted so easily to being addressed as Leopardi, instead of reacting angrily and rejecting its usage as he had once done.

But then his father never had understood him and never would. It was easy for Alessandro to accept the name now, because he no longer needed it to identify himself. In his estimation he was now a first amongst equals—more than an heir-in-waiting, and certainly more than any poor second son.

And yet, as Falcon had so succinctly reminded him when he had discussed the coming celebrations with him, he was still a Leopardi, and so far as Falcon was concerned that meant he still had a duty to the family.

Alessandro bore a grudging respect for his elder brother, but their relationship was shadowed by their childhood, by their father— and by the memory of Sofia.

But it was over a decade now since he had deliberately challenged Falcon in every way he could, engaging his elder brother in a power struggle, a battle to prove himself, which had ultimately resulted in them pitted against one another for the same woman—a struggle which Falcon had ultimately won.

Alessandro's frown deepened. He was not an insecure twenty-six-year-old desperate to prove himself any more. He was an adult, successful and confident, with no need to prove anything to his elder brother. Or to himself.

But wasn't it the truth that part of the reason he was so reluctant to attend tomorrow night's celebrations was because of those two words on the invitation: 'and guest'?

His pride insisted that he could not attend the celebratory ball without a partner, a fact his father would see as a sign of failure, and yet at the same time he knew that if there *had* been anyone in his life at the moment, sharing his bed, he would not have wanted to take her. Because he was afraid of a repeat of the humiliation he had experienced with Sofia. Alessandro knew that his reaction was irrational.

He knew too that by letting that irrationality take hold he was creating a self-perpetuating ogre within his own psyche. Perhaps his father had been right after all, he derided himself contemptuously. Perhaps he was a coward, and second rate.

At twenty-six he had been so proud to show Sofia, a model he'd met in Milan at a PR event—off to his elder brother, driven in those days by a single-minded determination to prove that far from being second best he could come first.

He had been flattered when Sofia had flirted with him. She had been older than him, twenty-eight to his twenty-six, and although he hadn't realised it then she had already been past the prime of her modelling career, and searching for a rich husband. Any rich husband, just so long as he was gullible.

It was easy for him to recognise now that what he had mistaken for love on his own part had merely been lust, and he knew too that he had much to be grateful to Falcon for. He had shown him just what Sofia had been—after all she was on her third husband now. Falcon had told him afterwards that the reason he had seduced Sofia away from him had been to show him exactly what she was, to protect him as it was his duty as the elder brother to do.

Without their father's love and protection it had been on Falcon's shoulders that the duty of protection for his younger siblings had fallen, and Falcon had taken that responsibility very seriously. Alessandro knew that. But the manner of his elder's brother's intervention had, in Alessandro's eyes, been humiliating—reinforcing the fact that he was second best—and it had left him with a cynical belief that all women would make themselves available to the most successful man they could find, no matter what kind of commitment they had already made to someone else, and could therefore not be trusted. Especially around his charismatic elder brother.

That belief had marked a changing point in his life, Alessandro acknowledged. Aside from the fact that he had taken care to ensure that his future mistresses did not get to meet his elder brother, he had also come to recognise that if he did not want to spend the rest of his life fighting to prove that he was worthy of more than being labelled a second son, and thus second best, then it was up to him to break free of the shackles that fastened him into that unwanted prison.

He had left Sicily for Milan, where he'd started up a small air freight business—ironically initially transporting the products of the city's designers to international shows. He had gone on from there to passenger flights and the separate luxury of first-class-only flights, so that now he had every aspect of the modern airline business covered.

He had even learned to use his second-son status to his own advantage. Membership of a titled family was something he used as cynically and deliberately as he used the powerful streak of sensuality he had discovered he possessed in the self-indulgent hedonistic months that had followed Sofia's defection.

The shell of the personality he had constructed for himself as Alessandro Leopardi was simply an image he projected for business purposes— an outer garment he could remove at will. Only he knew that somewhere deep inside himself there was still a vulnerable part of him that was the 'spare heir'—conceived only to fill that role, and of no value to anyone outside of that.

Alessandro could hardly remember their mother—she had died shortly after his younger brother Rocco's birth, when he had been only two years old himself. Everyone who had known her said that she had been a saint. Too saintly by far for her husband, who had spurned her and humiliated her publicly, turning instead to his mistress.

Did that same dark tide from his father's veins run within his own? Alessandro had no idea. He was merely thankful that, unlike his elder brother, he would never need to find out— because his own duty to the Leopardi name stopped well short of having to provide it with a future heir.

He removed a bottle of water from the suite's well-stocked bar and poured some into a glass. He could feel the stiff, unyielding thickness of the formal invitation jabbing his flesh in exactly the same way in which Falcon's stiff, unyielding determination that his brothers should pay their dues to their Leopardi blood jabbed his own conscience.

He and Rocco both owed Falcon a great deal. He had taught them and guided them, and he had protected them. Those were heavy duties for a young boy to have taken on, and it was perhaps no wonder that he had always imposed his own sense of duty on them—that he still did so now.

Alessandro didn't need to remove Falcon's letter from his pocket to remember what it said. Falcon never wasted words.

'Alessandro Leopardi,' he had written on the invitation, 'and guest'.

A challenge to him? Alessandro shrugged away the sharp pinprick of angry pride.

He would have to go, of course.

He was never comfortable when he had to return to the castle in Sicily where he had grown up. It held far too many unhappy memories. If he had to visit the island he preferred to stay in the family villa in town. Home for him now was wherever he happened to be—although he had an apartment in Milan and another in Florence, and a villa in a secluded and exclusive enclave close to Positano.

He looked at his watch, a one-off made especially for him. He would be leaving by helicopter from City Airport soon, for his own private jet and the onward flight to Florence, where he would stay at his apartment in the exclusive renovated *palazzo* that had originally belonged to his mother's family.

'Look, Leonora, I really don't think this is a good idea.'

Leonora gave her younger brother a scathing look.

'Well, I do—and you promised.'

Leo groaned. 'That was when I was halfway down one of Dad's best reds, and you'd tricked me.' He stood up, his brown hair tousled. He might be six foot three in his socks, but right now he still managed to have the frustrated look of a younger brother who had just been outwitted by his older and smarter sister, Leonora decided triumphantly.

'You agreed that the next time you flew your boss into London in the private jet I could fly him back.'

'Why? He hates women pilots.'

'I know. After all, he's turned my job applications down often enough.'

Leo's expression changed. 'Look, you aren't going to do anything silly, are you? Like barging into his office, telling him you flew the plane and asking him for a job? You'd have as much chance of succeeding as you would have of getting into his bed,' Leo told her forthrightly.

Leonora knew all about the stunning beauties the Sicilian billionaire who owned the airline her younger brother worked for dated, and she certainly wasn't going to allow Leo to guess how much his comment hurt—as though somehow it was a given that she wasn't woman enough to attract the interest of a man like Alessandro Leopardi. Not, of course, that she *wanted* to be one of Alessandro Leopardi's women, but she certainly did want to be one of his pilots.

'No, of course I'm not going to ask him for a job.'

Leonora crossed her fingers behind her back.

She was in full jokey can-do Leonora mode
now—even in the privacy of her own thoughts.
It just wasn't fair. She was every bit as good a
pilot as her younger brother, if not better, and she
just knew that if she proved that to Alessandro
Leopardi he *would* offer her a job. His exclusive
first-class service flew passengers all over the
world, and she wanted to be one of that elite
group even more than she had once wanted to
work for someone like Alessandro himself as a
private pilot.

'You can't possibly think you'll really get
away with this,' Leo protested.

'No, I don't think it. I know it,' Leonora told
him promptly, going on firmly, 'Since you let me
fly the new jet when you were sent to collect it
I've been having extra lessons in one, and I've
probably racked up more flying hours than you
have.' She didn't even want to think about how
much it had cost her to get those flying miles in
such an expensive craft, or how many lessons in
Mandarin she had had to teach to earn the money.

'Okay, so you can fly the plane. But you
haven't got a uniform.'

'Ta-dah!' Leonora said, opening her trench coat to reveal the uniform, and then producing her cap from the supermarket bag in which she had been carrying it.

Leo's face was a picture. 'You know if you get found out that *I'll* be the one losing my job.'

'Only wimps get found out,' Leonora replied as she slipped off her coat and swept up her hair before cramming it under the cap

'Captain Leo Thaxton at your service.'

Leo groaned again. 'Isn't it enough that you've stolen my uniform without stealing my name as well?'

'No,' Leonora told him. 'It's my name too. I've never had cause until now to be glad our parents thought it a good idea to give us practically the same name. Now, come on.'

'What about the co-pilot?'

'What about him? It's Paul Watson, isn't it? The one who breaks Alessandro Leopardi's rule about his pilots not partying with the stewardesses? I'm sure I shall be able to persuade him that it wouldn't be a good idea for him to say anything.'

'I knew I should never have told you about Paul. He's going to kill me.'

Ignoring him, Leonora demanded, 'Come on. I need you to drive me to the airport and get me through all the security stuff.'

'I do not know why you're doing this.' Leo groaned again, and then corrected himself. 'That's not true, of course. I do know why you're doing it. You are doing it because you are the most stubborn and determined female ever.'

'That's right,' Leonora agreed breezily. But inwardly she was thinking, *I'm doing it because I hate, hate, hate not getting what I want, and I want that job with Avanti Airlines more than I want anything else in the world.*

Yes, all of that was true—and when she was working full-pelt in her 'I'm up for anything' tomboy mode in front of an audience it was easy to pretend that the other Leonora—the one who longed for love and commitment, and to be allowed to be that other self she dreamed of— simply did not exist. At least for the length of her 'performance'.

She *did* want her dream job, of course, and she

certainly wanted the opportunity to challenge Alessandro Leopardi, to demand that he explain to her just why her sex weighed so heavily against her when she had such excellent qualifications. It was, after all, against the law to disqualify an applicant for a job on the grounds of their sex. There was no point in telling Leo about her plans, though. He would only worry. Better to let him think she was trying to make a point to him rather than planning to make Alessandro Leopardi agree that she was a good pilot and worthy of being given the job she craved so much.

CHAPTER TWO

IT HAD been a good flight, but then Alessandro had not expected it would be anything other than good. He had, after all, flown the new jet himself shortly after they had first taken delivery of it six months earlier, and had been very impressed with the way it handled.

Alessandro did not have his own pilot. Instead he preferred to use one of the pilots who flew his executive jets for the first-class-only service, because that way he got to ensure that they were maintaining the high standard he set for all those who worked for him.

Leo Thaxton was his youngest pilot, and today's flight had shown how well he was maturing into the job. Alessandro had particularly liked the way he had handled the small amount of turbulent weather they had run into halfway through the flight, smoothing the plane through it by taking it a little higher. Thaxton had shown good judgement there.

Nodding to the steward who was holding out his coat and his laptop for him, Alessandro left the aircraft. His car was already waiting for him on the tarmac, and he didn't so much as give the plane a backwards glance as his chauffeur opened the passenger door for him.

She had done it! Alessandro Leopardi couldn't say now that she wasn't good enough to fly his planes any more. Leonora felt almost ready to burst with triumph and excitement—only there was no one there for her to share her triumph with. Paul and the rest of the crew had left the minute Alessandro Leopardi had disappeared in his car.

She had booked herself into a small hotel in Florence and onto a returning commercial flight to London in a couple of days' time. Now that phase one of her plan had been completed she needed to move on to phase two, which was to confront Alessandro Leopardi in his office and persuade him to give her a job. It shouldn't be difficult now. She had the qualifications, and now she had proved that she had the skill as well. Plus, there was such a thing as legal equal opportunities, as she was perfectly willing to remind him should she need to do so.

They had only just reached the barrier to the private car park when Alessandro realised that he had left his mobile on the plane. Leaning forward, he instructed the driver to turn round and drive back.

Lost in her excited dreams, Leonora hadn't seen the car come back, or the door open, or Alessandro Leopardi get out as she left the plane, pulling off her cap as she did so to let her hair cascade down her back.

She saw him when she had reached the bottom of the gangway, though. Because he was standing there waiting for her, blocking her exit from it.

For a moment they looked at one another in silence. She was tall, but even standing on the steps she was still not quite at eye level with him and had to tilt her head back slightly to look up at him properly.

His question—'What is the meaning of this? Where is the pilot?'—was so icily cold that for once Leonora struggled to manage her normal flip tone.

'You're looking at her,' she told him.

He knew who she was immediately. After all he had looked at her many job applications often enough, and the photographs accompanying them. She looked far more sensually attractive in the flesh, with her hair worn loose. To his own disbelief, given the situation and his own normally unbreakable control over every aspect of himself and most especially his sexuality, he could feel his body responding to her proximity and that sensuality. Had he somehow known that she would affect him like this? Was that why he was so resolutely opposed to employing her? Of course not. He did not employ female pilots on principle—equal opportunities rules or not. Besides, he was Sicilian—and generally speaking everyone knew that Sicilian men had their own code of contact.

His eyes were so dark it was impossible to see their colour, and they were unreadable. But the slight flaring of his nostrils had already given away his rage. Leonora tried to clamp down on her sudden feeling that just maybe she had flown higher than she had planned. Her lungs certainly felt that the air was short of oxygen—or was that just her own apprehension?

'If that's true then you are in one hell of a lot of trouble—and so is Leo Thaxton.'

Alessandro Leopardi's harsh words confirmed that he wasn't about to treat her behaviour lightly.

'You can't blame Leo.' She immediately defended her brother. 'I made him do it. I wanted to prove to you that I can fly just as well as any man, and that I deserve a job.'

'What you and your brother both deserve is a prison sentence,' he told her mercilessly. 'And what you certainly will be doing is looking for a job together.'

Leonora's eyes rounded. This wasn't going the way she had planned at all.

'You can't sack Leo. It wasn't his fault.'

'Then whose fault was it?'

'Yours—for not giving me a chance to try out for a job,' she told him promptly.

Alessandro had never met anyone so infuriating or so reckless in ignoring the realities of the situation. By rights she ought to be treating him with kid gloves, not challenging him and arguing with him. He moved irritably from one foot to the other, reminded of the presence of the invitation in his pocket as its sharpness dug into his flesh.

The invitation. He looked at Leonora, and a plan began to form inside his head. She was attractive, if you liked her type—which he didn't. He liked groomed women, not girls with a mass of hair, too much attitude and too little sensuality.

'I most certainly can sack him, and I fully intend to do so,' he assured Leonora grimly.

He meant it, Leonora recognised. She could see that, and for the first time she realised that this wasn't a game she was playing. The consequences of what she had done were going to be very damaging—not just for her, but for Leo as well. Even worse was the mortifying recognition that, far from showing him that she could be the best, all she had done was prove that she was a failure.

Humiliation burned bright flags of red into her high sculpted cheekbones, highlighting the purity of her bone structure. She couldn't let him sack Leo. Apart from the fact that her brother loved his job, she could just imagine the comments that he and Piers—especially Piers— would make for the rest of her life, lording it over her as they so liked to do, because she was a girl and she had been born second.

Which would be worse? Swallowing her pride now and begging this man she would never see again to spare Leo, or facing her brothers as a failure?

She took a deep breath.

'I'm sorry. I shouldn't have done it. Please don't sack Leo.'

She sounded as though she was choking on every word, Alessandro recognised. Her brother obviously meant a great deal to her. *Good.*

'I will think about it. Provided you—'

Leonora's head jerked up immediately, her eyes shadowing with apprehension. Whatever it took to make sure Leo did not lose his job she would have to do—even if Alessandro Leopardi told her that she was never to apply for a job with him again. Even that, Leonora recognised bleakly.

'I'll do anything just so long as you don't sack Leo,' she interrupted fiercely. 'Anything! Whatever it is you want me to do, I'll do it.'

The moment her impetuous words were out, Leonora's mouth formed a self-conscious *O* whilst her face burned even more hotly as she realised just how her offer might be interpreted. However, before she had time to correct any possible misinterpretation, Alessandro Leopardi was speaking coolly.

'I won't sack your brother—little as he deserves to be kept on, in view of his stupidity and weakness in agreeing or allowing you to force him to agree to your illegal charade— provided you accompany me to a family function I am obliged to attend.'

Leonora stared at him, disbelief and distaste clearly visible in her expression. 'There are escort agencies who provide women for that kind of thing. Why don't you use one of them? After all, it isn't as though you can't afford to.'

She knew immediately that her blunt speaking had been a bad mistake. She could see the tinge of angry heat burning his face, moving into the high cheekbones and then flashing like a warning beacon in the darkness of his eyes.

'I would remind you that whilst I *could* afford to pay a woman to accompany me, *you* cannot afford to refuse me. Unless, of course, you are prepared to see your brother lose his job?'

To her chagrin his attitude caused Leonora to do something she hadn't done since she'd left her early teenage years behind her. She glowered at him and stuck out her bottom lip, with all the angry defiance of a rebellious teenager facing a resolute and immovable human obstacle to what they wanted to do. And then she compounded her regression to impotent resentment by saying crossly, 'Well, I can't think why you'd want to pick me to accompany you. After all, I'm not a model, or…or…a C-list starlet.'

Her face was burning again, but it wasn't her fault if his penchant for glamorous airheads was regularly recorded in celebrity gossip magazines—not that she ever bothered reading such things. It was Leo who was constantly pointing out yet another paparazzi photograph of his boss with some leggy, pouting beauty on his arm.

'The reason I've *picked* you, as you put it, has nothing whatsoever to do with your looks—or lack of them,' Alessandro told her unkindly.

This time she wasn't going to overreact, Leonora told herself. She was a mature woman, after all. A professional and fully qualified pilot. Someone who was not going to be tricked into behaving like an immature teenager because she couldn't control her own emotions.

'You are such a girl!' her brothers had loved to tease her when they had been growing up, and she still hated being put in a position where her emotions might threaten to make her look vulnerable or betray her.

'But you obviously want me to accompany you badly enough to blackmail me?' Leonora couldn't resist pointing out.

'That's right,' Alessandro agreed, so pleasantly and with such an unexpectedly warm smile that for a handful of seconds Leonora was caught off guard. And she found that for some inexplicable reason she was curling her toes in her navy-blue loafers.

He exuded an air of male virility that aroused

within her a raft of unfamiliar and complex emotions that undermined and weakened her. There was something about the way he turned his head, the look in the slate-grey eyes and the shape of his wholly male mouth that disrupted her ability to think logically and forced her to keep looking at him.

'You see, this way I shall have complete control over both the situation and you, without having to face any future comebacks—or indeed the kickbacks your sex has a less than lovable habit of demanding.'

'If you don't like the demands your girlfriends make on you then I would suggest that the fault lies with you and your judgement, and not my sex as a whole. There are any number of hetero-sexual women who don't ask for, or expect or even want anything from a man.'

'You're wrong about that. All women want something—either materially, emotionally or physically, and very often all three. Whereas all I want from you is your presence at my side in public as my partner, your recognition that in future there will be no relationship of any kind between us, and your complete silence on the whole subject—publicly and privately.'

'Not much, then,' Leonora muttered under her breath.

But he must have heard her, because he gave her a coldly arrogant look and told her, 'Set against your brother's future career, I would have said that it is not very much at all. Merely your absolute obedience to my will and to the instructions I shall give you for one single evening.'

'Like I said—that's blackmail,' Lenora was objecting, before she could stop herself.

'You may choose to see it as blackmail. I on the other hand see it as a justifiable claim for compensation from a person who has knowingly deprived me of something that is mine by right—in this case the skills of my employee, your brother.'

'I'm just as qualified as Leo—in fact I'm more qualified.'

'Maybe so, but you were not my choice of pilot. Now, as I was saying, if I am to refrain from sacking your brother then I shall require your complete obedience to my will.'

Her complete obedience to his will? Leonora

opened her mouth in a furious hiss of disagreement, and then closed it again as she remembered Leo.

There was one thing she had to say, though—one stand she had to make.

Holding his gaze, she told him bluntly, 'If this complete obedience to your instructions has anything to do with any kind of sexual activity then I'm afraid that Leo will have to lose his job.'

Alessandro looked at her in disbelief.

'Are you seriously suggesting that you think I am sexually propositioning you?' he demanded haughtily.

Leonora stood her ground.

'Not necessarily. I'm simply letting you know what I won't do.'

She had surprised him, Alessandro admitted. He was so used to women throwing themselves at him, practically begging him to take what they were offering, that it had simply never occurred to him that a woman like this one—so desperate to get a job with his airline that she was prepared to risk doing something that was both illegal and dangerous—would baulk at the thought of offering him sex. But patently that was exactly what she was doing, and he could see from the tension gripping her body that she meant what she had said.

Something—curiosity, male pride, his deep-rooted inherited Leopardi arrogance—Alessandro did not know which—spiked into life inside him, hard-edged and determined to make its presence felt. He shrugged it aside. Some ancient macho instinct had been aroused by her challenge—so what? He was mature enough, sophisticated enough, well supplied enough with all the sexual companionship he needed not to have to take any notice of it.

'Good. And now I shall let you know that you will never be asked. My standards in that regard, as in everything else in my life, are very high. You do not come anywhere near meeting them.' His smile was cruel and mocking as he went on coldly, 'I may be a second son, but I never, ever accept second best, much less third-rate. Now, since we have both made our position clear, maybe we can discuss what I shall require of you rather than what I most certainly do not?'

He had insulted her, but he could not hurt her, Leonora assured herself as she glared dry-eyed at him. She didn't care how third-rate he considered her to be sexually. In fact she was glad that he wasn't interested in her.

Alessandro pushed back the cuff of his shirt and looked at his watch. Why had he made that comment to her about his position as a second son? He didn't have to justify or explain himself in any way to anyone, never mind this irritatingly challenging woman who was the very last person he would have chosen to accompany him to the *castello* had he actually had any choice.

He could, of course, always go on his own, but that stubborn stiff pride that had driven him all his life insisted he had to prove to his elder brother that he could produce a woman who would not under any circumstances look at any other man— and that included Falcon himself. In that respect Leonora Thaxton was perfect, since he possessed the power to ensure that she would not do so.

He gave her a mercilessly assessing look, his mouth compressing. The raw material might be there, in the tumbled hair and the well-shaped face with its clear skin, but that raw material was in need of a good deal of polishing if his elder brother was not to take one look at her and, with a lift of that famously derogatory eyebrow of his, burst out laughing.

'Come,' he announced. 'My chauffeur's wife will be wondering where he is, and Pietro himself will be wanting his supper. My car is this way.'

Did he really expect her to believe that he was in the least bit concerned about his chauffeur or his chauffeur's wife? Leonora thought indignantly, as she was forced to run to catch up with him as he strode away from her, plainly expecting her to follow him to where she could now see a large limousine waiting in the shadows.

The chauffeur had the doors open for them as they reached the car, and Leonora's heart sank as she realised that she was going to have to share the admittedly generously proportioned back seat of the car with Alessandro.

As she sat down beside him on the tan leather seat he instructed her, 'You will need to give Pietro your passport so that he can show it at the customs office at the gate.' And then opened his laptop and ignored her, leaving her to seethe.

She handed over her passport, which was duly presented to the customs officer, but it was into Alessandro's outstretched hand that the chauffeur placed the returned passport once they were through the gate, not her own. Alessandro did not return it to her, despite the demanding look she gave him, choosing instead to slip it into the inside pocket of his jacket without so much as lifting his eyes from his laptop to meet her angry look.

CHAPTER THREE

'CATERINA will show you to the guest suite, and once you have refreshed yourself I will explain to you over supper the role I wish you to play. Since we shall have to leave Florence by mid-afternoon tomorrow we will not have much time, so immediately after breakfast we will address the matter of providing you with a suitable wardrobe for the weekend.'

'I have a change of clothes with me,' Leonora said, pointedly looking down at the small case which Pietro had placed on the marble-tiled floor of the elegant hallway in the two-storey apartment inside this eighteenth-century *palazzo* to which Alessandro had brought her.

Alessandro followed her gaze, and then swept his eyes from the case to the full length of her body and her face, with a comprehensive thoroughness that lifted the hairs on the back of her neck.

'And that change will be what? A pair of jeans and a shirt?'

'What if it is?' Leonora demanded

'The events to which I wish you to accompany me have been organised by my elder brother to celebrate and commemorate the granting to our family of its titles. They are not the kind of events at which guests will appear wearing jeans, which is why I am about to organise the services of a personal shopper who will ensure that you have the correct clothes.'

He began ticking the items off on his fingers, their lean, strong length somehow managing to distract Leonora to such an extent that she couldn't drag her gaze away from them. They were such very male hands, she thought, leaner and longer-fingered than the broader hands of her father and her brothers, tanned and with well-groomed nails, and yet here and there she could see small telltale white scars, as though the artistic streak revealed by the elegant length of his hands had manifested itself in a creative skill, but that of master sculptor rather than a painter.

'Tomorrow evening we shall be attending a cocktail party. And then on Saturday there will be an official luncheon party at the *castello*, with various civic guests of honour. In the evening there is to be a grand costume ball, and the celebrations are concluding with a special church service on Sunday.'

A cocktail party, a formal lunch, a costume ball and a church service. Leonora's heart sank further with every item Alessandro added to the list. She didn't have to search very far back in her memory to produce an unhappy image of the horrors of her one and only attempt at 'glamour' dressing, and the howls of laughter with which her brothers had greeted her appearance in the prom dress she had been persuaded into buying by a university friend for their finals ball. She just wasn't the pretty dress type—never mind the glam cocktail dress type. Whenever she did have to attend any kind of formal event she always stuck to a plain tuxedo trouser suit, with the jacket worn over a simple silk camisole top.

'I really think it would be much easier if you chose someone else to accompany you,' she felt obliged to say, her face burning when he looked at her in a way that made her feel as though she was piloting a plane that had just dropped ten thousand feet through the sky without any warning.

'I'm sure you do,' he agreed dryly.

'You must know dozens of women who would be more suitable.'

'That depends on how you define suitability,' he told her. 'Certainly I know many women who possess the sophistication and the beauty to carry off such a role, but, as I've already said, their compliance with my requirements would lead to them making demands for payment that I am not prepared to make. Whereas, whilst you may lack what they possess, I have the advantage of knowing that you will follow my wishes to the letter or risk costing your brother his job.'

'I can't see what can possibly be so important about accompanying you to a few social events that it necessitates a vow of absolute obedience and my agreement to your total control over that obedience.' Leonora chafed against his warning.

'I have my reasons for wishing to ensure that the woman who accompanies me to these events conducts herself in such a way that there can be no doubt in anyone's mind that she is wholly and absolutely committed to me and only to me, and at the same time also conducts herself with dignity and elegance—of manner and mind.'

'So a stunning Z-list glamour puss whose *modus operandi* involves going commando and drinking cocktails isn't high on your list of potential arm candy for this weekend, then?' Leonora guessed mischievously.

The manner in which he drew himself up to his full height and gave her a look that would have set Mount Etna alight if they'd been anywhere near it was certainly impressive, Leonora admitted. Her comment had certainly got under his skin.

'That kind of vulgarity is exactly what I do *not* want,' he agreed coldly, adding warningly, 'And that extends to the vulgarity of mind that gives rise to such comments.' He stared at her. 'Fortunately you are well educated enough to be able to converse intelligently with my brother's guests, and if you are asked about our relationship you will say simply that we met through your brother, who is one of my pilots. Falcon in particular will try to question you. My younger brother and I have good cause to be grateful to our elder brother for the care he gave us whilst we were growing up, and I must warn you that he will attempt to test you to see if you are worthy of me.'

When Leonora's eyes glittered with angry resentment, Alessandro shook his head.

'You are jumping to conclusions which are not valid. My brother's anxiety as to your worthiness has nothing to do with your social status. His concern will be to see that you will not hurt me, and it is on that issue that he will seek to test you, by hinting that he can offer you far more than I.' He frowned as his mobile purred, telling Leonora briskly before he answered it, 'We shall discuss all of this in more detail over supper.'

He turned away from her to take his call, leaving Leonora to look helplessly towards the magnificent wrought-iron staircase that soared up from the hallway to the upper floor. She was a reluctant eavesdropper on his conversation as he said coolly,

'Yes, I shall be bringing someone with me, Don Falcon. Her name?' He paused and looked at Leonora. 'Her name is Leonora Thaxton.'

Leonora's heart thundered with half a dozen heavy and dizzying beats. Hunger, she told herself pragmatically. That was all it was.

She focused on the cream marble of the staircase, which should have been so cold but somehow, in this Florentine setting, was a thing of beauty and sensuality that made her long to reach out and stroke the beautiful stone. Wanting to stroke the marble was fine, but she'd better not allow that longing to spread to wanting to reach out and stroke its owner, she warned herself— and then was thoroughly shocked that she should feel it necessary to give herself such a warning.

After all, why on earth would she want to touch Alessandro Leopardi, when she could barely tolerate being in the same room with him?

The only piece of furniture in the hallway was a large and ornate gilded table with a dark onyx top, on which sat a large alabaster urn filled with greenery and white lilies, their scent perfuming the air like a caress. Everything about the hallway made Leonora feel out of place and awkward, somehow underlining her own lack of sensuality whilst subtly highlighting its own. But was it the hallway that was making her so aware of her own lack of sensuality or Alessandro himself?

What if it *was* him? He could think what he liked about her—she didn't care, Leonora told herself stoutly, reverting to the defensive mechanisms she had learned as a girl. She didn't care one little bit as he finished his call and turned back to her.

A woman—Caterina, Leonora presumed—emerged from a door set at the back of the hallway. She gave Leonora a sharp look that whilst not exactly welcoming wasn't hostile either.

Alessandro addressed her in Italian, instructing her to take Leonora to the guest suite. Leonora, whose own Italian was excellent, was just thinking to herself that it might be a good idea not to reveal that she spoke Italian when Alessandro turned to her and said in that language, 'I seem to recall that your many job applications made mention of the fact that you are proficient in several languages, one of which is Italian.'

He had read her applications himself, and had still rejected her—despite the excellence of her qualifications? Rejected her as her brothers had so often done because she was female? Immediately and instinctively Leonora reverted to another of the habits of her childhood: wanting to get her own back. Without stopping to think she answered him in Mandarin, but the rush of triumph she felt was quickly destroyed when he spoke to her in the same language.

'Since Caterina does not speak Mandarin, I have to assume that your decision to do so is an exhibition of showing off more suited to a foolish child than an adult woman, and as such it reinforces my belief that you are not the kind of candidate who is suited to work for me,' he said coldly.

'Really? And to think I thought that it was my sex and my hormones that barred me,' Leonora retaliated sweetly.

'You've just underlined the reason for yourself—your immaturity,' Alessandro told her crushingly.

Why, why, *why* had she let that stupid childish

desire to show she was not just as good as but better than any male goad her? Leonora asked herself grimly. She turned away from him and spoke directly to Caterina in fluent Italian, earning the reward of a delighted smile from the older woman as she explained that she was Alessandro's housekeeper.

Five minutes later Leonora was earning herself another approving smile from Caterina as she gazed round the guest suite to which Caterina had taken her with awed delight.

The *palazzo* had obviously undergone a very sympathetic restoration and refurbishment process in the recent past, Leonora guessed as she admired the strong clean lines of the large, high-ceilinged rooms connected by a magnificent pair of open double doors. Whilst the elegance of its original plasterwork and ceiling cornicing and the beautifully panelled and carved doors had been retained, the walls had obviously been replastered, and were painted in an ivory that seemed to change colour with the light pouring in from the glass doors that led onto an ironwork girded balcony overlooking an internal

courtyard garden. Silver-grey floorboards reflected more light, and the room's mix of an
antique bed with pieces of far more modern furniture gave the suite an air of being lived in rather
than being a museum set-piece.

At the touch of a remote control Caterina
proudly revealed not just a flatscreen TV but a
computer, a pull-out desk and a sound system
discreetly hidden away behind a folding wall.

'Is good, *sì*?' she asked Leonora in English,
inviting praise of something of which she was
obviously proud.

'It is wonderful,' Leonora agreed, telling her in
Italian, 'It is a perfect blend of past and present—
a very *simpatico* restoration.'

Caterina beamed. 'This building and many
others belonged to the family of Signor
Alessandro's *mamma*, and so came to him and
his brothers. Together they have worked to keep
the family history but also to make it comfortable to live in now. Don Falcon, he sits on the
council that takes care of those buildings that are
owned by many of the old Florentine families,
and he makes Signor Alessandro pay much

money from his airline to help with the restoration work. Signor Alessandro knows that he cannot refuse his elder brother. Don Falcon has the most power because he is the eldest.'

'How many brothers and sisters are there?' Leonora asked her curiously.

'No sister. They are all three boys. Signor Alessandro is the second brother.'

The second brother—the second child, just like her. Leonora frowned. She didn't want to find any kind of connection between them, but as a second child he must have experienced, as she had, all that it meant to be a middle child, sandwiched between the lordly eldest and the favoured baby of the family, constantly having to fight for his position and for adult attention and love, never quite as good or grown-up as his elder sibling nor allowed to get away with as much as his indulged younger sibling. She wanted instead to continue to dislike and resent him. And besides, her situation had been worse—because she had been a girl sandwiched between two brothers. As same-sex siblings Alessandro and his siblings would have been able to bond together.

Or would he have had to compete even harder than she had done? Not that it mattered. She refused to start feeling sympathetic towards him. Look at the way he was treating her—threatening and blackmailing her...

Caterina had gone, giving her some time to freshen up before going back downstairs to have supper with Alessandro and receive her instructions.

In addition to the sitting room and bedroom, the guest suite also possessed a dressing room and a huge bathroom, with a sunken rectangular bath so large it could have easily accommodated a whole family and a state-of-the-art wet-room-style shower area.

Since it wasn't going to take her very long to get changed, Leonora allowed herself to be tempted out onto the balcony. Florence... Right now she should have been enjoying the magic of the city, making plans to visit all those treasures she wanted to see, instead of standing here, the captive of a man who was ruthlessly using her for his own ends.

It was dark outside, and all she could see of the

courtyard garden beneath her balcony were various small areas illuminated by strategically placed floodlights that revealed a long, narrow canal-style water feature, gravel walkways and various plants. There was a staircase from her balcony down to the garden, and as she stood on the balcony she could smell the scents of the night air and—so she told herself—of Florence itself.

Half an hour later, having showered and changed into her jeans and a top, she had just finished answering Leo's anxious text asking if all had gone well. She had given an airy and untrue response to the effect that there was nothing for him to worry about and that she was looking forward to her short break in Florence.

Caterina tapped on her sitting room door and then came in, announcing that she had come to escort Leonora back downstairs.

Several doors led off the hallway, and the one through which Caterina took her opened onto a wide corridor hung with a variety of modern paintings mingled with framed pieces of what Leonora thought must be medieval fabric and parchment. The whole somehow worked together in a way that once again made her feel acutely aware of the harmony of their shared composition.

At the end of the corridor a wide doorway opened onto a semi-enclosed loggia-type terrace, overlooking the courtyard garden, where Alessandro was waiting for her.

Like her, he had changed. What was it about him that enabled him to look so effortlessly stylish and yet at the same time so intimidatingly arrogant and sexually male? Leonora wondered on a small shiver. In profile his features reminded her of the profiles of ancient Roman heroes. She could quite easily imagine that close-cropped head wearing a laurel wreath. Her heart jolted into her ribs as though his compelling aura had reached out and somehow claimed her. She must not let him get to her like this. So he possessed both extraordinary male good looks and extraordinary male power? She was impervious to both. She had to be. That pumice-stone-grey gaze could not really penetrate her defences and see into her most private thoughts.

'*Grazie*, Caterina.'

He thanked his housekeeper with a smile so

warm that it had Leonora's eyes widening with surprise. This was the first time she had seen him showing any kind of human warmth, but she had no idea why it should have caused her such a sharply acute pang of melancholy. There was no reason why she should feel upset because he didn't smile like that at *her*.

'Since what I wish to say to you is confidential, and needs to be said in privacy, I thought it best that we eat here and serve ourselves,' he told her, as soon as Caterina had left, moving towards a buffet placed on a table against one wall, in which she could see an assortment of salads and *antipasti*. 'There are various hot dishes inside the cabinet. Are you familiar with Florentine dishes? Because if you wish me to explain any of them to you then please say so.'

Going to join him, Leonora marvelled. 'Has Caterina prepared all this?'

Alessandro shook his head.

'No. Normally when I am here in Florence I either eat out with friends or cook for myself, but on this occasion I ordered the food in from a nearby restaurant.'

'You can cook?' The gauche words were out before she could silence them, causing him to arch an eyebrow and give her a look that made her feel even more self-conscious.

'My elder brother insisted that we learn when we were growing up.'

Alessandro spoke of his elder brother as though he had parented them, and yet Leonora knew that Alessandro's father was still alive.

Ten minutes later, with her main course of *bistecca alla fiorentina*, a salad dish of sundried tomatoes, olives and green leaves, and a glass of Sassicaia red wine in front of her—which Alessandro had explained to her was made from the French Cabernet Sauvignon grape—Leonora could feel her mouth starting to water with anticipation. Her appetite, though, was somewhat spoiled when Alessandro began to outline what he expected from her in return for not firing Leo.

'As I have already said, the celebrations and ceremonies of the weekend will be of a formal nature, during which, as my father's second son, I shall be expected to play my part in representing the Leopardi family. Family is important to all

Italians, but to be Sicilian means that the honour of the family and the respect accorded to it are particularly sacred. If Falcon allowed him to do so my father would still rule those who live on Leopardi land as though he owned them body and soul.'

Because she could hear the angry loathing and frustration in his voice, Leonora fought not to speak her mind.

'Falcon, when the time comes, will guide our people towards a more enlightened way of life, as our father should have done. But all his life our father has controlled others through fear and oppression, none more so than his sons. Now in the last months of his life, he expects us to give him the love and respect he delighted in withholding from us as the children of his first marriage, while he lavished everything within him on the woman who supplanted our mother and the son he never let us forget he wished might have supplanted us. Some might think it a fitting punishment that he has had to live through the death of both of them.'

Leonora was too shocked by Alessandro's revelations to hide her feelings. The delicious food she had been eating had suddenly lost its flavour.

'He must have hurt you all very badly.' That was all she could manage to say.

'One cannot be hurt when one does not care.'

But he *had* cared. Leonora could tell.

'It is important that you know a little of our recent family history so that you will understand the importance of the role I wish you to play. During his lifetime our halfbrother, Antonio, was our father's favourite and most favoured child. In fact he loved him so much that when, on his deathbed, Antonio told our father that he believed he had an illegitimate son, he insisted that the child must be found. Not for its own sake, you understand, but so that he could use it as a substitute for the son he had lost. Falcon was able to trace the young woman who might have conceived Antonio's child.'

'And the baby?' Leonora pressed, immediately fearful and hardly daring to ask.

'The child was not Antonio's. Although as it happens he will be brought up as a member of the Leopardi family, since my youngest brother is now married to the child's aunt. My father is so obsessed with Antonio that initially he refused to accept that the child was not his, but, as Falcon has said, it is just as well that there *was* no child. If there had been our father would no doubt have repeated the mistakes he made with Antonio and ruined another young life. Had there been a child I would certainly have done my utmost to ensure that it remained with its mother, and that both of them were kept safe from my father's interference in their lives.'

He meant what he was saying, and Leonora was forced to admit that she could only admire him for his stance.

He moved slightly, reminding her of a dangerous animal of prey, dragging her thoughts away from the child whose potential fate he had described so compellingly and to her own unwanted vulnerability—to him. But then she saw the expression in his eyes as he gazed beyond her, as though looking back into his own past, and she recognised that he had his own vulnerabilities. He too had once been a small child—lonely, afraid, needing to be loved and protected.

She saw his mouth and then his whole expression harden, all his past vulnerability overridden by sheer will as he told her, 'These days I consider myself fortunate that I was our father's least favourite. The one he liked to humiliate the most by reminding me of the fact that I had been given life merely to be a second son whose usefulness would come to an end the day Falcon produced his own first-born son.'

As a second-born child herself, Leonora had thought she knew what it meant not to come first, but the cruelty Alessandro had just revealed so unemotionally was horrific. So much so that she had started to reach across the table towards him, in an instinctive gesture of comfort, before she realised what she was doing, quickly curling her fingers into her palm and withdrawing her hand, her face burning when she saw the frowning, dismissive way his gaze had followed her betraying movement.

'To his credit, Falcon did his best to protect both us and himself. I have a great deal of respect and admiration for my elder brother, and all three of us share a bond that is there because, young as he was, he took it upon himself to ensure that we stood together and supported one another.

My father thought to continue to control us all into adulthood through the loyalty we bear to our family name and of course through his wealth. But, whilst Falcon insists that the Leopardi name is accorded loyalty and respect, we have all three of us in our different ways made ourselves financially independent and successful as ourselves, rather than as his sons. Even me—the son he labelled second-born and second-rate.'

Leonora took a deep gulp of her wine in an effort to suppress her unwanted surge of aching sympathy for him.

'Of course in my father's eyes no man can consider himself to be a true man unless he has succeeded beyond all other men in every aspect of his life. My younger brother is married. But since Falcon is the heir, there is no woman alive that he could not, if he wishes to do so, command and demand as his wife. Were I to attend the weekend's celebrations without an appropriate female partner then my father would no doubt publicly and repeatedly claim that for all my financial success I am a failure as a man. I cannot and will not allow that to happen.'

How well she understood that need to prove oneself, Leonora admitted to herself.

'Your father is hardly likely to be impressed by *me*,' she felt obliged to point out.

'You underestimate yourself.'

She stared at Alessandro in astonishment, whilst something warm and sweet and wholly unexpected unfurled tentatively inside her heart—only to wither like life in an oxygen-deprived stratosphere as he continued.

'It is not, after all, your looks that matter. Any fool can buy the company of someone who currently passes for a beautiful woman, and most fools do. You, on the other hand, have a certain authenticity that comes from your lack of plastic prettiness which, allied to your qualifications, make it more rather than less likely that we could share a relationship. My father sees and understands only what he wants to see and understand. Falcon, however, is not so easily deceived—which is why you will remain at my side at all times and not allow yourself to be drawn into any kind of private conversation with my eldest brother.'

'If you want me to act the doting adoring girlfriend and cling to you like a limpet, then I'm sorry but—'

'What I want you to do is behave as any intelligent, sophisticated and self-confident woman would—with dignity and grace to which you will add total and absolute loyalty of a type that speaks discreetly rather than loudly of your devotion to me.'

He reached for the bottle of wine and held it out to her, but Leonora shook her head, afraid that if she drank any more wine she might be tempted to tell him just what she thought of the prospect of having to pretend to be devoted to him—either discreetly or loud. Even so, she couldn't resist saying sweetly, 'You won't want me displaying this loyalty by saying that it would be a good idea to skip the socialising and go and have sex instead, then, I take it?'

The look he gave her was hard-edged, with a mixture of warning and contempt.

'Only the immature believe that sexual vulgarity is attractive. And besides, no woman of mine has ever needed to *ask* me to take her to bed. You will not speak with, flirt with, dance with or disappear with anyone else. If asked, you will say that we met through your brother, and you will remain charmingly and discreetly vague about the length of time we have known one another, and the nature of our relationship and its past and future, referring anyone who asks about it to me. You will behave towards me as though you are proud to be with me and as though you love me. As an example you will, for instance, place your hand on my arm and look intimately at me, making clear to others that there is no man on this earth you would rather be with who could take my place in your heart and your life.'

'So I don't have to do much, then?' Leonora couldn't resist saying.

'You are the one who put your brother's career at risk.'

'But you are the one who is blackmailing me into playing a role that is totally abhorrent to me,' Leonora retaliated. 'If I did love anyone then it would be a love born of mutual respect and commitment. Not some…simpering, adoring, dutiful hero-worship thing. And if I wanted to give the man I loved a look in public that said

I wanted to go to bed with him, then he would be pleased and proud to drop everything to do just that.'

'That may have been your experience with previous lovers.'

'My experience is nothing whatsoever to do with you.' And nor was her lack of it, thank goodness, Leonora acknowledged, recognising that the conversation was beginning to move into a potentially hazardous area.

Somehow she doubted that Alessandro Leopardi was a man who would understand why a woman of her age was as lacking in sexual experience as she was other than to say that such a lack reinforced his already low opinion of her. It couldn't be easy for him, she decided, having to depend on her to play what was obviously an important role so far as he was concerned when he disliked and despised her so much.

'If you really want my acting as your besotted but *über*-discreet love interest to work then you're going to have to behave publicly as though you *want* me in that role,' Leonora pointed out to Alessandro.

'It will be enough that I have asked you to accompany me.'

For sheer arrogance he really took the prize, thought Leonora in disbelief.

She could hear a bird singing in the courtyard, and she turned to look towards it, commenting, 'Your garden looks lovely.'

'But I must warn you it is out of bounds,' Alessandro informed her. 'And I must ask you not to go into it. Now, I shall run through everything with you again, just to be sure that everything is understood. Tomorrow morning, after breakfast, you will be taken to acquire a suitable wardrobe for the weekend. Your measurements will be taken and sent to a theatrical costume agency in Milan, which will supply a costume for you to match my own and fly it direct to Sicily. Immediately after lunch we shall leave for Sicily. I shall fly us myself on this occasion. My brother will greet us on our arrival at the *castello*, and you will be welcomed formally as my current lover.'

'How are you going to explain my disappearance so immediately after the weekend is over?' Leonora asked him curiously.

'Easy. I shall have discovered during the course of the weekend that you were beginning to bore me.'

'I'm not surprised,' Leonora couldn't resist saying. 'I'd be in danger of expiring from boredom myself if I was really anything like the dull creature you seem to think so perfect.'

CHAPTER FOUR

IT MIGHT be midnight but she was still wide awake—and the forbidden garden below her balcony was really too tempting to resist. All the more so because it was forbidden. What harm could it really do for her to go down the stairs and just take a look? None at all. Alessandro was obviously the kind of man who liked making rules for the sake of it, in order to flaunt his power.

The matching strapless top and three-quarter-length bottoms of the leisure suit-cum-sleepwear combo she was wearing were practical and re-spectable enough for her to go down into the garden, and if Alessandro should happen to see her then so what? He was hardly going to do anything, was he? He needed her compliance over the weekend too much to lock her up in a dungeon, or whatever it was his ancestors had done to those who annoyed or opposed them in any way.

As she negotiated the narrow flight of wrought-iron stairs Leonora mused that it was puzzling that, whilst Alessandro so evidently admired his elder brother and felt grateful to him, at the same time he did not trust him enough to confide in him about his planned deceit— which ostensibly he was carrying out because of his father.

Since they were both middle children, Leonora tried to imagine herself in his position. Piers had never been her protector in quite the same way that Falcon Leopardi appeared to have been Alessandro's, so that wasn't quite the same. She did love her brother, though. But she had felt sharply aware of being the only non-partnered one of the three of them the last time they had all been at home together, she reminded herself.

She had reached the garden, but she didn't move into it, stopping instead to digest the reality of her own admission to herself. That was not the same as what Alessandro was planning to do, though— and anyway, his elder brother did not have a partner. She didn't know why she was bothering to try to understand what was motivating him, anyway. He didn't deserve her sympathy.

She wandered into the garden, intrigued by the formality of the long, narrow canal.

'Arrgghh—'

The sudden shock of spurts of icy-cold water hitting her from every direction had Leonora screeching in shock, trying to dodge out of the way of the jets that were soaking her clothes and her hair with ever-increasing force.

'I warned you not to come down here.'

A firm hand closed round her wet arm, ruthlessly yanking her away from the canal and through the darkness of the garden to another set of stairs.

Soaking wet, her teeth chattering, Leonora complained, 'But you didn't warn me that you'd set up a booby trap for me in case I did.'

'Don't be ridiculous. The water jets are the reason I told you not to use the garden. They were at one time a traditional feature of Renaissance Italian gardens, installed to amuse their owners and soak unsuspecting guests. These are undergoing some restoration work, which has resulted in an inability to turn off the jets whilst new parts are awaited.'

'If you'd told me all of that in the first place then I'd never have come into the garden.'

'My warning should have been enough. To anyone other than a woman who insists on behaving like a rebellious child it would have been.'

He was still holding on to her, and Leonora pulled away from him. Her movement activated a security light, which burst into life, illuminating the marble paved area on which they were standing, a statue clinging lovingly to a basket of grapes—and the fact that the shirt which Alessandro had been wearing during dinner was now plastered to his torso and that her own drenching had resulted in her leisurewear turning completely see-through.

Leonora's panicky squeak combined with her frantic attempt to move back into the shadows brought an audibly impatient exhalation from Alessandro's grim, downturned mouth.

'Your modesty is risibly unnecessary,' he told her bluntly. 'Even if you were the most desirable woman I had ever met, and I had spent the entire evening anticipating taking you to bed, the sight of you right now would have dampened my ardour even more thoroughly than the water jets have done your clothes. What on earth *are* you wearing, by the way?'

'It's leisure and sleepwear,' Leonora answered.

'Appalling. The only thing a woman should ever sleep in is her lover's arms or her own skin.'

Right now the unpleasantly clammy embrace she was enduring was beginning to make her shiver and long for one of the huge, thick, fluffy towels she had found in her *en suite* bathroom, Leonora decided.

'Well, now that we've both agreed that we don't turn one another on, and that a bit of un-planned alfresco sex is out of the question, would you mind telling me the fastest and driest route back to my bedroom?'

By the time she had finished speaking she was shivering so much her teeth had started to chatter.

He, on the other hand, looked predictably ar-rogantly handsome—the victor surveying the spoils of war with a contemptuous downward glance at her from beneath deliberately dropped eyelids. The light fell cleanly on the pride-honed sculpted flesh of his cheekbones and the hard masculinity of his jaw. A shudder of something she could neither control nor understand jolted through her.

'This way,' Alessandro told her, gesturing towards the stairs. 'It's a bit of a long way round, but it will be dry.'

The steps went up to a balcony much wider than her own, complete with a table and chairs, and to an open door through which she could see a starkly and magnificently male bedroom, illuminated by a modern chandelier of driftwood and silver.

Leonora looked at Alessandro, and then at the room, and then back at him, resisting the firm pressure of his hand in the small of her back as she hung back a little, and said foolishly, 'But that's your bedroom.'

'Correct. It is also the only way you can get to your own room without going back through the garden.'

He sounded exasperated and irritated, but

Leonora had now become distracted by the delicious warmth spreading out through her body from his hand against her back. If she leaned into it the warmth would increase and spread further, reaching right down to her toes, for instance, and up to her…

'This is all your fault,' she accused him. And it certainly was—because no one else had ever made her feel that she wanted to soak up the warmth of their touch in such a blatantly sensual way.

'You were the one who initiated it.'

Stung by his claim, Leonora whipped round and defended herself indignantly.

'No, I wasn't. You were the one who touched me. *Oh*!'

Oh, indeed. It was obvious from Alessandro's expression that they were at cross purposes, and Leonora's face flamed as his gaze, which had been fixed grimly on her face, slid down over her body, resting deliberately on the full thrust of her breasts against the wet fabric of her top. Its intensity was somehow, and quite shockingly, causing her nipples to tighten into aching peaks, making her want to wrap her arms protectively around her body to conceal their betrayal.

This really wasn't a good idea, Alessandro warned himself. She wasn't his type—and anyway, her temporary role in his life was better remaining strictly business. But her ridiculous comment had caught his sense of humour, and her breasts *were* absolutely delicious—would be even more so without the top that was clinging to them, covered instead by his hands, their hard, flaunting nipples caressed by his lips and his tongue… What harm could it really do? In fact it could only add authenticity to their roles.

Alessandro was going to touch her, kiss her— do something more than that, perhaps. Leonora panicked and backed into the bedroom.

Alessandro followed her, his hunting instincts aroused.

'You said you didn't want me,' Leonora reminded him as he reached for her and drew her towards him with one lazy movement of his arm.

'*You* said you didn't want *me*,' he taunted her, rubbing his nose erotically against her own in a way that sent a jolt with the power of a dozen jet engines surging though her body. His words were a whisper as soft as morning clouds against her lips, as he added meaningfully, 'And you lied.'

Leonora sucked in her breath, a dozen furious objections on the tip of her tongue. But Alessandro's tongue was tracing the shape of her mouth, and its intimacy shocked her into a heart-thudding silence. Any thought of doing verbal battle with him had been vanquished. Any thought of doing anything at all was an impossibility, she admitted helplessly as the soft, teasing stroke of the experienced male tongue suddenly became a determined thrust that took advantage of her weakness. She clung on to Alessandro's shoulders for dear life as the dizzyingly swift ascent of her response to the sensual possession of his kiss took her so high that she felt as though she was suffering from oxygen deprivation.

How could such an argumentative, awkward, irritating woman cling to him as though helpless beneath the sensuality they had ignited? How could she melt into his arms and into his kiss as though they were what she had been born for?

And how could he be stupid enough to respond to her reactions like some raw, crass boy who had never known a woman's arousal before?

Alessandro didn't know. What he did know, though, was that her response was inciting him to push aside her wet top and then span her narrow ribcage with his hands, deliberately tormenting himself by delaying the moment when he slid them upwards to hold the soft weight of her breasts, splaying his fingers against them, rubbing her nipples with the pads of his thumbs, feeling the jolt of pleasure that rocked through her body and hearing the sharp, almost shocked moan she sobbed against his kiss.

At the sound of her arousal pleasure ricocheted through him. He wanted more—her naked body in his arms, beneath his hands and his lips, her cries of need filling his ears in the hot, secret darkness of his bed. He wanted to know her and enjoy her and fill her with a pleasure and a satisfaction that would be unique within her sexual experience. She had challenged him, and now, having done so, she had totally undermined the hostility he had felt, with the sheer sensuality of her abandoned response to him, like honey after vinegar, stealing from him his resistance to her.

And he must resist, Alessandro recognised. He must resist or face the consequences. There was no place in the purpose for which he was allowing her into his life for any kind of intimacy between them—least of all this kind.

Alessandro could feel the resistance of his body to his thoughts, but he was not a man who allowed physical needs—of any kind—to dominate his actions.

Alessandro had stopped kissing her, Leonora recognised. He had stopped touching her too, and was stepping back from her, leaving her to shiver, bereft of his body heat. The night air touched her damp clothes and naked skin.

'So,' Alessandro announced calmly, 'now that I have indulged your sexual curiosity, perhaps I should remind you of my warning to you earlier about the role I expect you to play? It is a role that does not and will not—ever—require your presence in my bed.'

He had indulged her sexual curiosity? Leonora's face burned. She wasn't the one who had kissed him or pushed up his top and touched him. No, but she was the one who had responded to his kiss and quivered with open longing beneath the experienced touch of his hands on her breasts.

'You were the one who brought me here,' she told him fiercely.

'And you were the one who was curious.'

Leonora opened her mouth to deny his accusation, and then closed it again. Could she honestly put her hand on her heart and say that she had *not* been curious about what it would be like to be kissed by him, a man so far outside her own circles and way, way outside her personal experience? But surely it was only natural that she should have wondered? Wondering, though, did not mean that she had actually wanted him to kiss her. Had she? Not beforehand, perhaps, but once she had felt the warmth of his breath on her lips and the touch of his hands on her body, hadn't she wanted more?

'I'd like to go back to my room, if you could point me in the right direction?' she told Alessandro, desperate to escape from her own thoughts as well as from him and his too-knowing questions.

Nodding his head, he answered her. 'This way.' Striding across the bedroom and then into a large open-plan sitting-room-cum-office, he turned to look at her, frowning before telling her briskly, 'Wait here.'

What else could she do? She had no idea how to find her way back to her room, and she certainly didn't fancy wandering all over the apartment dressed as she was, in a still very damp leisure suit.

He wasn't gone long, returning carrying a large taupe-coloured bath towel, which he tossed towards her saying, 'You'd better wrap this around you,' before going to open the door and waiting for her to join him. 'Follow this corridor until you reach the stairs, then go past them and continue down the next corridor. You room is the first door on your right.'

Thanking him, Leonora hugged the towel around herself and made her escape.

That was the trouble with women, Alessandro told himself as he returned to the work he had been doing before he had seen Leonora in the garden. They just could not resist giving themselves the ego boost of getting some man—any man, more often than not—hot for them.

He sat at his desk, frowning as he re-read the e-mail he had found in his in-box earlier. His concierge service apologised, but the stylist they had found for him had cancelled, and they weren't able to replace her with a substitute of equally high calibre. That left him with two options: to trust Leonora, or accompany her himself.

No man of his wealth and position could get to the age Alessandro had without the experience of being coaxed, coerced, sweet-talked and seduced into accompanying beautiful women to expensive and exclusive designer shops—especially if they were Italian. And besides, sometimes it was easier and speedier to end a relationship that had served its purpose with a goodbye gift of a few designer outfits as a sweetener.

Not that there had been anyone sharing his bed for the last year—or longer. Which was no doubt why Leonora Thaxton had had such an unexpected and powerful effect on his libido. His pride might not like the fact that she had aroused him but, looking at things from a more practical point of view, the fact that they had shared a handful of minutes of pre-coital sexual intimacy at least meant that there was a familiarity between them now, which could only work to his advantage in public. In private there would not be a repeat of that intimacy—that went without saying.

But back to the matter of providing her with a suitable wardrobe—and quickly… His frown deepened, and then eased as he searched though his e-mail addresses until he found the one he wanted. Cristina Rosetti was one of a certain top-flight designer's right-hand women, and she owed him a favour, having had to ask him once or twice to arrange for models to be flown to New York when their original travel arrangements had fallen through at the last minute. Several designers used his airline to freight their priceless one-off pieces of clothing around the world to private and public showings, but he had known and liked Cristina for several years—on a strictly business basis.

CHAPTER FIVE

LEONORA woke up slowly and reluctantly, trying to hang on to the protective ignorance of sleep whilst she fought against the growing feeling of panic and apprehension that waking up was bringing.

By the time she had opened her eyes she had total recall of the events of the previous day, and her heart had sunk to the depths of the hollowed-out, aching space that was her chest. She looked at her watch. Half past eight? She sat bolt-upright, pushing her tangled curls out of her eyes. How could it be that late? She was always up early. It must have been her dread at what lay ahead of her today that had kept her protectively asleep and oblivious.

She wasn't either of those things any more, though. She wondered what time she was being collected to be taken shopping for clothes suitable for the weekend's events—and, of course, suitable to meet the high sartorial standard he no doubt required of his female companions. Leonora pulled a face at herself. She hated the restrictions of 'result' clothes. She was strictly a casual-clothes woman.

She heard the outer door to the suite opening and tensed—but it was only Caterina, bringing in her breakfast.

'*Buon giorno*, Caterina,' Leonora offered with a warm smile, getting out of bed and looking appreciatively at the selection of food on the tray, which included what looked like home-made muesli as well as the ingredients of a more traditional continental breakfast and—most important of all—a jug of fragrant-smelling coffee.

Leonora contemplated the personal shopper who would be accompanying her as she tucked into her muesli. Stick-thin, probably, and dressed like someone out of *Sex and the City*—either that or one of those fearsomely elegant women who populated the designer outlets of the more upmarket parts of London. Leonora had seen them from outside the shops, on her way to give private Mandarin lessons to her wealthy clients.

Oh, yes, she was quite happy to think about what lay ahead of her—but what she was not happy to think about was what had happened last night. How could she have responded to Alessandro Leopardi in the way that she had? Wildly, passionately, and as though she had actually *wanted* him to kiss her. When the reality was that he was the kind of man—sexually experienced, predatory, too macho, too much of all things male—that she would normally have taken one look and fled.

When it came to sex they were not even in the same league table, never mind sexually matched. When she thought of how she had lived for so long with a dread of being publicly exposed and then ridiculed as an inexperienced virgin, neither wanted enough by a man to be swept off her feet and into his bed, nor having ever wanted any man enough to encourage him, she felt positively ill at the memory of what she had done last night. Just imagining the humiliation she would have suffered if Alessandro hadn't stopped when he had, and had gone on to discover her shameful secret, was enough to make it impossible for her to eat another mouthful of food because of the sick churning in her stomach.

Why, why, *why* hadn't she done what virtually every other girl she knew had done and unburdened herself of her wretched virginity at university? Because she had been too busy fighting to out-do her brothers, that was why. How much simpler her life would be now if she had focused instead on losing her virginity. Taking a rest between lovers because one was focused on forging one's career was understood and accepted by others. But never ever having had sex was a social embarrassment of huge proportions, and something that rubbed painfully against Leonora's always easily stung pride.

She had thought that the person she most dreaded finding out was probably Leo, but now she recognised that Alessandro had replaced Leo as the man she would least like to know of her embarrassing virginity. If Alessandro had continued to make love to her last night how long would it have been before he had guessed?

Would something in her response have given her away, or would he have only realised later?

Whatever the answer to that was, she had no difficulty at all in imagining what his reaction would have been. Leonora guessed that as a middle child, a second son who had obviously been emotionally scarred by his father's cruelty to him, his pride would have objected to the idea of bedding a woman no other man had wanted to bed. He would have seen her as a reject— even an oddity, perhaps—and he would have recoiled from her because of that. A man like Alessandro would always be driven to acquire and possess that which other alpha men either craved or already possessed. That went with the territory of having been the child he had and having become the man he was.

Just as she was trapped in her tomboy image, so he was equally trapped in his drive to be first, and to have the best. The difference between them, she suspected, was that whilst she as an adult very often disliked the persona she had created to protect the child she had been, finding it wearisome and immature, Alessandro *liked* his alter ego.

Leonora rarely allowed herself to dwell on such profound and personal thoughts. They cut too deep and exposed too much—especially at times like this. She didn't want to be marooned in the tomboy girl she had taught herself to be in order to compete with and excel against her brothers. Her brothers had unwittingly reinforced that role, keeping her in it within their family make-up. Out of pride and stubbornness she had remained the eternal tomboy rather than admit to those who knew her best that she longed to be recognised as a woman; she was afraid to ask them for the help and acceptance she needed to retrace her steps to the point where the tomboy should have slipped naturally away and the woman should have taken her place in a natural girl-to-woman transformation.

There was no point in her wondering what she should wear, she acknowledged now, putting aside her unproductive and uncomfortable soul-searching, since it would have to be her jeans. Somehow she didn't think that the stylist was going to be impressed by them.

* * *

Alessandro watched from the shadows of the hallway as Leonora came down the stairs, his body disobeying his head with its unwanted and irritatingly juvenile immediate response to her. Despite her ill-fitting jeans and loose top he was sharply aware that beneath them she possessed lushly sensual breasts and a waist so narrow that any red-blooded man would instinctively want to span it with his hands. She was long-legged too—something that no doubt Falcon, whose women were always tall and leggy, would immediately notice.

This morning the tangled curls were constrained in a thick plait, which showed off her cheekbones and the fullness of her mouth. He hadn't thought of her initially as a beauty, much less as a woman possessed of alluring sensuality with the power to arouse a man against his better judgement, but now his body was reacting to her as though she were all of those things, and in doing so it was forcing Alessandro to acknowledge a potential and very unwanted complication to his plans.

When he had blackmailed her into agreeing to

his plans the thought that he might find her sexually attractive had been the last thing on his mind. Alessandro was scrupulous about not mixing business with pleasure. He had seen what happened to others when they did and he had no intention of allowing his own life to become inconvenienced by the toxic effect of extricating himself from a sexual relationship he no longer wanted with a woman with whom he was involved in another area of his life.

Not, of course, that he was saying he was in danger of becoming sexually involved with Leonora Thaxton. He was, after all, a man who prided himself on his control over himself. He was simply annoyed with himself for initially letting the fact that she had managed to win his approval for her flying whilst deceiving him as to her identity blind him to her sexuality.

Leonora came to a wary halt at the bottom of the stairs. When Caterina had informed her that she was to go down to the main entrance to the apartment once she had finished her breakfast, she had hoped that the only person she would meet there would be the stylist—not Alessandro Leopardi.

Stepping out of the shadows, Alessandro announced coolly, 'There has been a change of plan. I shall now accompany you myself.'

Leonora knew that her indrawn breath was both audible and a betrayal of her feelings. An indignant flush of colour stained her face. She also knew that Alessandro wouldn't care how much she objected to his change of plan. But maybe after he'd told the stylist about her she'd refused point-blank to take on such an unrewarding challenge, Leonora thought with black humour.

'As most of the better-known designer stores are here on Tournabouni Street, we may as well walk rather than risk being stuck in the city's traffic.'

Leonora was feeling too dispirited to respond as she compared the way she was going to be spending her precious time in Florence with the way she had planned to spend it—visiting museums, exploring the streets and enjoying the timeless ambience of the Medici city.

Even though it was only just gone nine o' clock in the morning there was already a warning strength in the sun, where it fell in slats of gold from the side streets. Tournabouni Street was a busy thoroughfare, bordered by imposing buildings, many of which had been converted into designer stores. Their doors were closed to shoppers at this early hour of the day—but not, apparently, to Alessandro, as Leonora discovered when he stopped outside one exclusive shop and then removed his cell phone from the inside pocket of the elegantly cut linen jacket he was wearing over a striped shirt and a pair of jeans far better cut than her own.

He texted something swiftly, speaking to her without looking up. 'I have told Cristina, who will be here to take charge of you in a minute, that you are to accompany me to Sicily and that you have lost your luggage in transit—'

He broke off as the door opened and a stunningly elegant woman stepped out to embrace him with a warm, '*Ciao*, Alessandro.'

As he kissed her on both cheeks, he told her, 'I shall forever be indebted to you, Tina.'

How many women must he have brought here in order to merit the store being opened early for him? What did it matter to her how many there had been—and what was the cause of that sudden fierce flash of painful anger? Not jealousy, Leonora assured herself.

'Well, we owe you several favours, Sandro, for getting the models to New York for us in time for the last collection's show.'

So perhaps it wasn't because he bought clothes for his lovers here that the store had been opened. If that was relief Leonora was feeling it was only because she didn't want anyone thinking that she was one of his women.

'Here is Leonora, Tina,' Alessandro was saying, 'I shall leave her in your capable hands.'

After another very Italian embrace between them he was gone, striding down the street, leaving her feeling curiously bereft when she ought to have felt relief, Leonora admitted, as Cristina beckoned her inside, and then relocked the door.

'It is every woman's dread that her clothes disappear, no?' she sympathised with a swift shrug. 'Before we started to use Alessandro's cargo service every time we pack for one of the international clothes shows, I am—what do you say in England?—on needles until I see that all is well and everything has arrived.'

'On pins,' Leonora told her, with a smile that Cristina returned. She was older than Leonora, in her late thirties or maybe her early forties, Leonora guessed, but so elegant that it was hard to put an exact age on her.

'I have brought with me some of the stock from Milan, as we have things there that we do not have here in Florence, and also a hairdresser and a make-up artist, since Alessandro tells me your work has meant that you have not been able to visit a proper hairdresser for some months.'

If by a 'proper hairdresser' Cristina meant the kind of hairdresser who charged a fortune and with whom it was impossible to get an appointment, then her 'some months' should have been 'ever,' Leonora admitted ruefully. It would take more than designer clothes and an expensive haircut to transform her into the kind of woman Alessandro normally dated.

But then he wasn't dating her, was he? she reminded herself as she followed Cristina down a long white-walled corridor that curved and then straightened before opening out into a white space furnished with low black chairs and a black table.

As though by magic two black-suited young women suddenly appeared, folding back a section of the white 'wall' to reveal neatly hanging and folded clothes.

'We will start, I think, with the basics. Jeans— which you will need for Sicily, especially if you plan to do any sightseeing around the Etna area—worn with perhaps a blazer and a silk shirt, and some fine knits as an alternative.'

As Cristina spoke the two girls were removing clothes from the rails and placing them on one of the chairs.

'You will, of course, want to create the right impression when you arrive—you are tall, and so can get away with trousers. I think this pair in neutral cream will be perfect. Here is this cardigan to go with them, and this silver necklace with the matching cuff—very smart. And for the cocktail party I have brought this from Milan.'

Leonora's eyes widened as she gazed at the

lilac and grey layers of silk chiffon that made up a short dress with a bubble hem and a fitted strapless bodice, and at the neat fitted jacket that was worn over it. It was beautiful—but not for her. She never wore clothes like that. She didn't have what it took to carry it off.

Shaking her head, she told Cristina regretfully, 'It's lovely, but I don't think it's really me.'

'We will try it and see,' Cristina said, overruling her.

Two hours later, exhausted and bemused, Leonora stood in front of a mirror and caught her breath in disbelief at her own reflection. Her hair was newly cut, in a style that seemed to consist of a mass of shiny sensual layers where once had been a tangle of too-thick curls, and it seemed somehow to emphasise her cheekbones and make her eyes look bigger. Her bare shoulders rose from the silk chiffon cocktail dress, whilst her eyes—thanks to the clever application of make-up—seemed to glow a smoky violet colour. The dress made her look fragile and feminine in a way she had never imagined she could look.

'It is perfect for you,' Cristina pronounced, looking pleased. 'I knew it would be when Alessandro described to me your colouring. This gown, and the cream silk satin full-length gown you must also have—you have the perfect figure for them. The jeans also, and the trousers. You have the long legs that look so good in them.'

Leonora wasn't going to argue with her. She had never imagined that she could look so good. She even felt confident about wearing the bright acid-yellow cotton sundress that Cristina had insisted was a 'must' for sightseeing daywear, along with the pair of skinny-legged jeans which could be rolled up to Capri length. There were also a couple of outrageously expensive T-shirts, along with a gorgeous silk parka in pewter-grey, to tone in with the whites, silvers and greys of her other new 'casual' clothes.

Both evening dresses had their own matching shoes and clutch bags, and she'd been given a make-up lesson to go with the designer cosmetics that were to replace those she had 'lost in transit.' She also had a large, soft and squishy 'daytime' bag, that worked with both the trousers and the jeans.

After instructing one of the girls to unzip the cocktail dress for Leonora, Christina had left her alone in the fitting room. Leonora couldn't help delaying the moment when she removed the dress, as she stood in front of the mirror and marvelled again at the transformation it had effected. For the first time she saw an image of what she could be—all that she had secretly longed to be since she had left her university years behind. Now she saw in the mirror a woman who was hardly daring to hope, as yet not entirely comfortable with her new image, looking back at her. The beginning of the woman that she could become—a woman at ease with herself, confident about her ability and her right to be both vulnerable and strong, to be both feminine and capable of holding down a demanding job in what was still in many ways a man's world without having to compromise herself.

It was one of the pretty black-suited young salesgirls who told Alessandro where he could find Leonora. Having assumed that he and

Leonora were lovers, she omitted to mention that Leonora was alone in the private changing suite, so that when he walked in, his arrival masked by the thickness of the dove-grey pile carpet, Leonora was oblivious to his presence.

Alessandro, because of the angle of a long pier glass mirror in the lounge area off the changing room, and because Cristina had fastened back the curtain, was perfectly able to see and study her. Anyone witnessing his reaction could have been forgiven for thinking that he was not pleased with what he saw, since he had started to frown.

The reflection in the mirror showed him a stunningly beautiful young woman, wearing an elegant dress that suited her to perfection. But it was the look in Leonora's unexpectedly violet-tinged eyes that was responsible for his frown, not her appearance. Alone, and unaware that she was being watched, she wore an expression so open and revealing that it was an intimacy he didn't want to have—one that rolled his heart over inside his chest, seizing it in a tight fist of compassion streaked with an angry awareness of the knowledge of what he could see so plainly in her face. She looked like a little girl, scarcely able to believe in her own luck, delighted and yet at the same time struggling to balance between something she desperately wanted and some long-held inability to believe she was worthy of such joy.

Leonora could feel her eyes burning with very private tears. She tried to blink them away, and then felt laughter bubbling in her throat as she realised she couldn't wipe them away without ruining her new make-up or risking getting it on her beautiful dress, since she didn't have a tissue to hand… Holding the dress to her, she turned round, remembering that there was a box of tissues on the coffee table in the lounge area— and then froze as she saw Alessandro.

Even if he hadn't already been able to see that her emotions had nothing whatsoever to do with the acquisition of an expensive gown and every-thing to do with something very private within herself, Alessandro suspected that the intensity of her shocked reaction to his presence would have convinced him on that point.

How long had he been there? He couldn't

have—must not have seen her looking at herself in the way that she had. She could not have borne for anyone to see that, but most of all not him. Her face began to burn, her old tomboy-style defences springing into action.

Not a man who was used to putting the emotional needs of others first, Alessandro surprised himself when he heard himself saying calmly, as he backed out of the room, 'Sorry—I didn't realise that you weren't ready.'

Leonora's relief was so intense that it dizzied her. He had not seen her. If he had he would not have been able to resist saying something. She knew that from what she had experienced at his hands—and, of course, from her experience of growing up with brothers. She knew other girls who had brothers, of course—some of those girls were eldest sisters and some of them youngest, and their experience did not mirror hers. The elder sisters often mothered their men, and the youngest ones always seemed to attract men who were protective of them and indulgent towards them.

Just as Leonora was nodding her head, not

trusting herself to speak, Cristina reappeared, clicking her tongue when she saw that Leonora was on her own and still wearing the cocktail dress.

CHAPTER SIX

SO MUCH had happened that it was hard to accept that it was less than twenty-four hours since she had come down these steps, Leonora admitted as Alessandro stood to one side to allow her to precede him up the steps to his private jet.

This time, instead of wearing her pilot's uniform, she was dressed in her new clothes: designer jeans encasing the slender length of her legs, stiletto heels on her feet and a plain white T-shirt that had cost the earth. Personally she thought it clung far too neatly to her breasts, which was why she was wearing a butter-soft leather jacket over it, despite the heat of the Italian afternoon. Expensive designer sunglasses and the new soft leather bag completed her outfit; the whole look was one that was almost a uniform for well-bred and well-to-do women—one that could be found from Fifth Avenue to Knightsbridge, taking in Paris and Milan on the way.

Below her she could see her new matching leather luggage—white with tan straps, and a logo so small and discreet that it could only be found by the *cognoscenti*—being loaded, along with two more masculine and rather more travelled versions.

She had been taken off guard when Alessandro had announced that he would be flying them himself to Sicily, and even more surprised when he had informed her that she would be in the cockpit with him, as his co-pilot.

'Not that you will be doing anything other than acting as a non-flying co-pilot,' he had told her emphatically.

'You didn't have any complaints about my handling of the jet when I flew you out from London,' Leonora had felt defensive enough to point out. 'And I *am* a fully qualified pilot.'

'For the moment. Had anything happened, the fact that you were illegally flying the plane would have made the insurance null and void, and that alone would have been enough to ensure that you were stripped of your licence for a very long time.'

His warning had sent a cold chill of apprehension icing down Lenora's spine—and not just because of the threat it had contained. He had made a legitimate point that she, in her determination to prove herself, had overlooked—and it stung her pride that he should have spotted her error and pointed it out to her.

Ascending the steps into the jet behind Leonora gave Alessandro ample opportunity to take in the neat curve of her bottom in the new jeans, as well as the length of her legs. Even with heels on she was still several inches shorter than him and, unlike her bulky borrowed and adapted uniform, her jeans showed off her curves and her femininity.

Although he wasn't going to say so to Leonora, the main reason he had decided to fly the jet himself, with her in the co-pilot's seat, was that he didn't want to arouse the curiosity of his pilots over how or why he was suddenly squiring around the sister of one of their number. For another thing, he wouldn't put it past Falcon to start asking some typically awkward questions as to why, since Alessandro and Leonora shared a passion for flying, they had not shared the intimacy of that passion coming out to Sicily. Falcon knew how much he hated handing over control of anything he could do himself to anyone else, and it was part and parcel of his elder brother's analytical and protective nature to ask far too astute questions when he suspected that something was being withheld from him.

Had someone told her twenty-four hours ago that she would be seated in the co-pilot's seat of Alessandro Leopardi's private jet, with Alessandro himself at the controls, Leonora would have been so filled with excitement and triumph at the thought of getting to show him the excellence and capability of her skills that she would have been overjoyed. But twenty-four hours ago she hadn't known what she knew now, having met Alessandro Leopardi.

Now she had. Leonora risked a quick, brief look at his profile whilst his attention was focused on the pre-flight checks, her heartbeat suddenly speeding up to a heavy drumroll. Her heart itself did a series of back flips that threatened to leave her severely deprived of oxygen. Speedily Leonora transferred her gaze to his hands, but far from being a safer option this too resulted in her heart doing a spectacular loop the loop as for her eyes only, her memory ran an inner video of those hands on her breasts.

It was all very well telling herself that a bit of role playing would not go amiss, given what lay ahead, but there was certainly no need for her to take things that far, Leonora told herself, hastily reaching for her own headset, ejecting the seriously disruptive images from her head so that she too could concentrate of the pre-flight checks.

He had been right to make it a rule never to employ female pilots, Alessandro decided, as the scent of Leonora's skin mingling with the perfume she was wearing intruded between him and his focus on the familiar pre-take-off routine. And the distraction of her smell was second only to the soft thrust of her breasts beneath the white T-shirt now that she had removed the leather jacket she had been wearing. There was no need to ask him just why it was that the visual impact of natural breasts was so much more effective than the solid unmoving thrust of pumped-up silicon.

If she had removed her jacket in some kind of attempt to soften him up for a fresh attempt to persuade him to give her a job she had made a very big mistake. No way, having felt the impact the sight of that soft jiggle was having on his own body, was he going to risk exposing his pilots to it.

Flying a plane demanded total concentration. Not the distraction of the sight and scent of a sexually alluring woman.

It was warm inside the cockpit, and Alessandro had removed the linen jacket he had been wearing when they boarded the plane. His shirt, short-sleeved and casually open at the throat, pulled against the breadth of his back when he leaned forward, making Leonora foolishly catch her breath and fight to suppress a soft squirm of pleasure at the memory of how it had felt to have the breadth of his shoulders and the heat of his flesh beneath her hands. Today his torso might be covered by the cotton of his shirt, but last night the dampness had moulded cloth to flesh, allowing her to see quite clearly the structure of his muscles and the darkness of his body hair, somehow dangerously erotic in comparison to the waxed torsos of the male models favoured by advertising campaigns.

Guiltily Leonora looked away and felt her face and then her whole body overheat as she realised that in her haste to avoid looking at his torso she had inadvertently allowed her gaze to drop down to the open spread of his legs. Not that she could actually see anything—well, only that he was a man, of course. But it just wasn't the done thing to stare at the male crotch. Or at least it wasn't *her* done thing, but now…

Her mouth had gone dry, and her heart was pounding too fast and too unevenly. Somehow she managed to drag her gaze away, her guilt sending her lurching into a frantically fast burst of speech as she asked, 'How long is the flight?'

Too long for the kind of intimacy the flight deck was imposing on him, Alessandro admitted to himself, as he shifted slightly in his seat to ease the ache he could already feel pulsing in his groin.

'An hour—less if we get a tail wind.'

Leonora nodded her head vigorously, to mask

the horrified embarrassment she felt at the way in which Alessandro was moving his body as though in warning against her intrusive visual attention.

A voice crackling in the headphones from air traffic control brought her back to reality, and years of training enabled her to focus on what she should be doing.

They had been in the air for less than fifteen minutes when Leonora had been forced to admit to herself that Alessandro was a first-rate pilot—superbly skilled technically, and in absolute control of both himself and the aircraft. But now, with Sicily spread out below them, offering herself and her beauty up to them, Alessandro's flying skills were taking second place to Sicily's beauty. The sight of Mount Etna, so dangerous and yet so compelling, made her reflect on how well suited Alessandro was to the land of his birth.

'If you look to the east now you will see the *castello*.'

His unexpected advice had her eyes widening and her breath catching with dismay as well as awe when she saw the size of the castellated fortress on a rocky outcrop, separated from an equally medieval walled town by several acres of olive trees. Beyond the town the land rose towards the mountains, and here and there a small cluster of buildings clung to their steep sides.

Alessandro frowned as he looked down at the mountain villages below them. His father ruled his lands and those who lived on them with a feudal mindset he refused to relinquish. He might like to think of himself as a patriarch revered by his people, but the truth was that he was more of a despot. There were children living in the remote mountain villages on Leopardi land whose families were so poor that they were still forced to leave school to work on land for which they still had to pay Alessandro's father a tithe.

Falcon had sworn to abandon the practice once he inherited, but in the meantime there was unrest in one of the villages in particular. Alessandro's sympathies lay entirely with the villagers, but at the moment it was the absorbed, marvelling look on Leonora's face that caused him to circle round so that she could have a better view.

Their shared role on the flight deck had been

unexpectedly harmonious—a good omen for the weekend and for his determination to ensure that everyone, but most of all his father, would be forced to recognise that there was nothing and no one he could not have exclusively to himself if he chose to do so.

After a textbook-perfect descent onto what Alessandro told Leonora was his own private airfield, the jet hummed gently to a halt. Sharp bright sunshine burned down onto the runway, turning it blindingly white under a pure blue sky.

The first thing Leonora noticed, as she stepped out onto the steps rolled into place by immaculately turned-out ground staff in overalls bearing the Avanti Airlines logo, was the scent of citrus mingling with the hot, acrid smell of aircraft fuel, exhaust fumes and hot metal. The heat of the sun, so much stronger here than it had been in Florence, had her reaching immediately for her sunglasses and mentally thanking Cristina for warning her that she would need a hat to protect her head if she went out in the heat of the day.

Some men were unloading their luggage, and Alessandro had joined her on the metal platform at the top of the steps. As they stood together in silence, an immaculately polished limousine, with a small pennant fluttering on its bonnet, slid through the dusty afternoon to come to a halt with its passenger door exactly in line with the steps. A uniformed chauffeur emerged from the driver's seat and went to open the rear passenger door, facing them. The man uncoiling himself from inside the car was tall and dark-haired, and his physical resemblance to Alessandro was unmistakable as his air of authority, Leonora recognised.

Uncertainly, but automatically, she turned to look at Alessandro. She could see his chest expand as he breathed in and then exhaled with perfect control, and his mouth was chiselled and hard as he told her in a clipped voice, 'It seems that Falcon has come to welcome us in person.'

Falcon. The name suited him, Leonora acknowledged. Every bit of him exuded an aura that spoke of total power allied to total self-control, underscored with something that suggested that he could be very dangerous if provoked. And yet for all his power and good looks he did not send her heart into freefall, or force the muscles of her lower body to clench in agonised denial of the intimate sensual ache he had caused in them, in the way that Alessandro could and did.

Leonora found herself reluctant to descend the steps. Because she didn't want to be here and was being forced to do so? Or because she feared that the man standing impassively waiting for them might see through their deceit and Alessandro would punish her for that by sacking Leo?

Without realising what she was doing she backed into Alessandro, trembling slightly as she did so. Automatically he reached out to steady her, placing his arm round her waist and turning her into his own body, holding her so that she was practically leaning against him, the hard muscles of his thigh pressed between her own jean-clad legs.

Leonora felt shock seize her breath, causing her to tremble even more at the unexpectedly sensual intimacy of his hold. She was torn between pulling back and—shockingly—wanting to lean closer, to be closer, to bury her face against his shoulder so that she wouldn't have to face the scrutiny of the man waiting for them.

Panic filled her. She gave in to it, turning her face towards him as she whispered shakily, 'I can't do it. He—your brother will know. I...'

Alessandro's arm tightened round her.

He should be used by now to the effect his elder brother had on women. There was no real reason why he should feel such a fierce, primeval surge of male possessiveness. He felt nothing for Leonora, after all, and she would be a fool to risk her brother's dismissal by flirting with Falcon.

'Falcon is merely a man, not a magician. He cannot read minds or hearts, no matter how much he sometimes wants others to believe that he can. Like any other man he will believe what he sees—and this is what he will see.'

He pulled her closer and bent his head, and her eyes betrayed her as she looked up at him, offering him free access to her lips as though she wanted his kiss. His hand cupped the side of her face. To protect her from the sun and his brother's gaze or to hold her captive? Alessandro didn't know—and as soon as his mouth covered hers he discovered that he didn't really care.

Why was it with this woman that where there should have been suspicion, the belief that she was putting on an act to entice him, instead the sensation of her mouth trembling with excitement beneath his own made him believe in her, made him feel both powerful and vulnerable? And so aroused that he was drawing her in close against his body and holding her tighter, deepening the kiss, probing that soft, trembling mouth mindlessly and seamlessly, for all the world as though he had her to himself and they were alone in a place where nothing mattered other than the way she was making him feel.

This wasn't real. It was a role Alessandro was playing—that was all. Leonora tried to remind herself, but her body wasn't listening to her mind. Instead it was reacting to the fact that she was in the arms of a man who was kissing her with fierce, compulsive desire. But Alessandro did not desire her, and she must not let her mouth soften under his or her body melt into his. She must not put herself in a position where she could and would be humiliated and hurt.

Hurt?

It was the frantic trembling of Leonora's body and the agitated pressure of the hand she lifted to his chest to push him away that wrenched Alessandro back to reality.

As soon as he released her Leonora started to descend the steps, panicked by the shock of recognition that Alessandro could hurt her. How had that happened? How on earth had she managed to become emotionally involved in any kind of way with a man she had known less than twenty-four hours? But it wasn't the quantity of time she had spent with him so much as its quality. Their intimacy, both cerebral and sensual, had brought her closer to him than she had ever been with any other man. From the moment he had stopped her as she left the plane he had occupied every single one of her thoughts, full-time.

Gripped by her unwanted discovery Leonora forgot about her high heels and gave a startled gasp as she caught one of them on the steps and started to fall forward.

Strong arms caught her and held her safe—but they were not Alessandro's arms. Her body knew that immediately, and thus she was able to relax into them without fearing what it might betray.

Falcon Leopardi was as tall as Alessandro, and as broad, but where Alessandro possessed a fierce, sensual intensity that strobed danger into her senses, Falcon had an unmistakable air of right and of acceptance of that right, in a way that reminded her of her own elder brother. He was plainly at ease with himself and his position. His magnetic dark-eyed gaze sweeping her from head to foot—not merely in a man's assessment of her but also that of an elder brother checking her out to see if she was good enough for Alessandro.

She felt safe with him, Leonora recognised. But she would only be safe as long as he believed that his brother was her first priority.

'I'm sorry. So silly of me. I forgot that I was wearing high heels,' she apologised as she eased back. He immediately released her.

'Well, well—and what have I done to deserve the reception, Falcon?'

Alessandro's voice, sarcastic and cynical, came from immediately behind her, sending her heart jerking against her ribs as though he was holding it on a string.

'Is there any reason why I should not be the first to welcome you home? And, of course, Miss Thaxton with you.' Falcon's smile for Leonora was brief but warm as he turned to her and said, 'You must have impressed Alessandro if he allowed you to co-pilot the plane.'

'Leonora doesn't need to impress me with her flying skills. It is her absolute loyalty to me for which I value her,' Alessandro told his brother, slipping his arm round Leonora's waist and drawing her close to him. He looked down at her and reached with his free hand to brush a stray hair off her face, then rubbed his thumb across her lower lip, caressing the curve of her waist as he did so, as though he was totally unable to stop himself from touching her.

He was giving such a good performance of a man besotted with her that even Leonora herself was impressed. But what was the purpose of the deliberate challenge he had thrown down to his brother with his comment about her loyalty? It hinted at a rivalry between them that at some point had gone deep and still festered—at least on Alessandro's part. Was that the reason for his demand that she show him absolute loyalty and devotion as 'his woman' over the course of the weekend?

Somehow, without even having to make a deliberate decision to do so, she was automatically trying to imagine how *she* would have reacted had she had an older sister and there had been a contest between them over a boy. The rush of emotions that gripped her told their own story—anger, fierce anger, against both the boy and her sister. But the real scalding heat of that anger would have been directed at her sibling, along with a ferocious need not just to show her that she could find another boy who would not be tempted by her but find one who would be far, far better than the one she had lost.

Was that why Alessandro had blackmailed her into being here?

'I hope my brother has managed to be practical enough to explain what this weekend is about, Leonora, and what is going to take place?'

Falcon's calm voice broke into her inner specu-
lations and forced her to put them to one side.

'Oh, yes,' she was able to assure him truthfully. 'Alessandro has been through everything
with me.' Well, that much was true…

'It was kind of you to come down and welcome
us, Falcon, but rather a waste of time. I prefer to
drive us back to the *castello* myself, since I'll
need my car whilst I'm here. I've promised
Leonora that I'll make time to show her something of the island.'

That was news to her, but Leonora managed
not to betray her surprise.

'I've already arranged for your car to be driven
home for you,' Falcon assured Alessandro
smoothly.

An elder, superior sibling, reminding a
younger and inferior one that he was ahead of
him in every way and always would be? Or was
she reading too much into their exchange? It
wasn't like her to allow herself to become so
involved in the dynamics of another person's
family relationships—she was normally far too
busy being defensive about her own—but some-

where deep inside her a tiny seed of fellow feeling for Alessandro had taken root, and much as she wanted to be able to do so she couldn't ignore it.

'The shared drive back together will enable me to get to know Leonora a little better,' Falcon was saying smoothly, turning to Leonora herself as he added, 'Your brother is one of Alessandro's pilots, I believe, Leonora?'

'My younger brother—yes,' Leonora agreed, adding, 'Like Alessandro, I'm a middle child. Something else we share—like our love of flying.'

Now, why had she said that? As though she was making a point and taking a stance, declaring not just her loyalty to Alessandro but the fact that she felt they shared a special bond. She could see the frowning reception Alessandro was giving her statement, and wished she had not been so impulsive and spoken out so forcefully. It wasn't as though Alessandro needed her to make a stand on his behalf. They weren't a proper couple, after all—one for all and all for one, facing the world together utterly united.

And now Falcon was looking at her very thoughtfully indeed, and Alessandro's frown had grown deeper.

It was Falcon who ushered her towards the chauffeur, who was waiting for them to get into the car. Although he had initially got out of the back seat, now Falcon got into the front passenger seat, leaving Alessandro to sit behind him whilst Leonora sat behind the chauffeur.

'Alessandro will, I am sure, have informed you that since he is the only one of the family attending the weekend's events to have a partner, you will be looked upon by many of our guests as their hostess.'

Leonora gave Alessandro a frantic look. He had certainly *not* told her that.

Ignoring the look she was giving him, but reaching for her hand and holding it in what looked like a lover's clasp but which was in effect, Leonora suspected, a warning grip, he told his brother, 'Leonora is more than capable of playing her part, Falcon.'

Leonora suspected that both his words and his grip on her hand were intended as a reminder to her of the control he had over her and the obedience he expected from her.

The drive to the *castello* didn't take very long—barely long enough for Leonora to take in the olive groves through which they were being driven, which gave way to a more barren landscape as the road climbed upwards, with the sea to one side of them and the mountains to the other.

Finally, after the road curved round one of the mountains, she could see the *castello* up ahead of them—not so much clinging to the sheer rocks on which it was built as gripping them in its talons like a bird of prey. Despite the sunlight warming the steep escarpments and the crenellated walls, Leonora shivered slightly. The sight of the *castello* filled her with the sense that it was designed to intimidate and overwhelm, to entrap and imprison. It was, she decided, a true fortress—hard, unyielding and hostile. Like Alessandro himself.

When they drove through a stone archway into a large flagged courtyard that contained an ornate fountain, Leonora saw not the medieval castle building she had been expecting but the elegant façade of a magnificent eighteenth-century palace. She could not stop herself from gasping in surprise.

It wasn't Alessandro who responded to her astonishment but Falcon, turning round in his seat to smile at her and tell her, 'One of our ancestors had the good sense to replace the original buildings. All that is actually left of the original *castello* are the outer walls and a couple of towers. Which reminds me, Sandro, I've told Maria to put you both in the West Tower Suite, to give you a bit of privacy. As you can imagine, the house is going to be packed to the rafters with guests, so I thought you'd be more comfortable there than in your old room.'

What did he mean, he'd put 'them' in the West Tower Suite? Leonora wondered in an apprehensive silence. She looked at Alessandro, but he wasn't looking back in her direction, and now wasn't the time to start asking Alessandro exactly what their sleeping arrangements were going to be, Leonora acknowledged.

As they climbed the steep marble steps leading

to impressive double doors, Leonora realised that she was going to struggle to climb them elegantly in her unfamiliar high heels. Unexpectedly, as Alessandro hadn't seemed to notice the anxious look she had given him in the car, he did seem to notice she was having trouble with the steps, because without saying anything he placed his hand beneath her elbow to steady and support her.

For a second the tomboy in her wanted to insist she could manage, but tomboys didn't wear stilettos, and the truth was that she was glad of his help. The last thing she wanted to do was make a fool of herself by falling flat on her face. But climbing the steps so close together brought her thigh into contact with his, sending a frisson of something that quite definitely did *not* belong to her tomboy days sizzling through her body.

'You're the first to arrive,' Falcon was saying. 'Officially the cocktail party begins at seven, with dinner for the house guests at ten, but Father is planning to hold court at around six, although I want to keep that as low-key as possible, given his poor health.'

'Is his heart as weak as we've all been told? Or

is it just another of his ploys to make us all jump through hoops of his making?'

When Leonora heard the bitterness in Alessandro's voice she instinctively started to move closer to him, in a mute gesture of comfort and support—and then abruptly stopped. Why on earth would Alessandro want comfort or support from her? And, even more to the point, why should she want to offer them?

To her relief he appeared not to have noticed her instinctive movement towards him, although his hand had slipped from her elbow along her back, and was now resting on her hip, which had brought her closer to him. But he had not so much as looked at her, his focus entirely on his brother.

'His heart condition is real enough,' Falcon was saying. 'I would have preferred not to have risked worsening it with all this fuss, but he insisted, threatening that if I did not organise something then he would do so himself.'

'And his word, of course, is law,' Alessandro said cynically.

'He is the head of our family and our name, and it is—as it has always been—our duty to respect the traditions and the responsibilities that go with being a Leopardi.'

'You may respect him if you wish to do so, Falcon, but I never shall.'

'I did not say that I respected him. What I said was that it is our duty to respect our responsibilities to our name. Not for our own sake, and certainly not for the sake of our father, but for the sake of our people. It is their traditions that we are honouring this weekend, not our father's.'

They had reached the top of the steps now. Both men were standing still, facing one another, and Alessandro still had his arm around her waist, securing her to him. It was just because of the role she was forced to play that she was not objecting to that imprisonment, Leonora assured herself.

'You sound as feudal as he is, Falcon, and you know my views on that,' Alessandro told his brother.

'Yes. You say you are a modern man, who does not bow his head to anyone or expect them to bow to him. That is all very well for you, Alessandro, but many of our people do not think as you do.

And if we ignore and insult our heritage then in effect we ignore and insult them as well.'

'It is thanks to our father that they have been kept in the Dark Ages and treated like serfs—exactly as he tried to treat us when we were young. I can never and will never accept that. You know that. In my opinion our true duty and responsibility is to free our people from the feudal yoke our father has no right to continue to impose on them.'

'I agree. But for some of them—the older ones— that freedom is feared because it means change.'

'I am glad I am not in your shoes, Falcon, and that as our father's heir the responsibility for righting his wrongs is yours and not mine.'

'A fitting punishment for being born first, Sandro? We are all born to our given roles in life and we have no power over that. What we do have power over is how we choose to deal with that role. You have chosen to show the world that you do not and will not accept any limitations imposed on you by others in any way. But you are still a Leopardi. We still share the same blood—'

'Our father's blood,' Alessandro interrupted him bitterly.

'The blood of many generations of our name.' Falcon overrode him. 'Your example will show our people that they need not accept any limitations, whilst the duty I have shown our father will, I hope, enable the younger ones to make the transition to a more modern way of life without riding roughshod over the older generation. It is my wish that we use this weekend to set an example of all that is good and just and honourable about being a Leopardi.'

Falcon Leopardi spoke less assertively than Alessandro, but there was no mistaking the determination of his purpose, Leonora recognised. He was very much the eldest sibling, very much making it plain that his will would prevail, and yet at the same time he was also showing true respect and brotherly love for Alessandro. But would that ever be enough for a man like Alessandro, who was so obviously driven by a need to come first? Would he ever be content with what he had achieved? Or would he always feel that it was not enough because he had not been born first?

The huge double doors had been opened whilst

the brothers had been talking, and now they were walking through them together. Alessandro was keeping her close to his side.

The hallway beyond the doors had obviously been designed to impress and awe, with its richly painted and frescoed ceiling, its ornate gilded rococo decor and the huge glittering chandelier that dominated the curving stairway. The whole area breathed power and wealth.

Another set of double doors stood open, giving visual access to not just the room beyond them but to an entire series of rooms, their doors also flung open, with sunlight illuminating intricately inlaid wooden floors. This wasn't a home, Leonora decided, it was a statement of intent— a kingdom in its own right.

Falcon looked at his watch.

'It's four o'clock now. I dare say you'll want to take advantage of the chance to relax and settle in while you can, so I'll leave you to take Leonora up to your suite, Sandro, and then we can meet in the library at five-thirty, just in case there are any last-minute changes to any of the arrangements that we need to discuss.'

'This way.' Alessandro turned her round so that they were facing the main doors, guiding her through them and across the courtyard to a narrow door in the wall. 'It's quicker than going through the main house,' he explained, as Leonora looked uncertainly at the spiral of stone steps leading upwards in the half-light coming in through the narrow slits in the bare stone walls.

On impulse she removed her shoes, answering the look Alessandro gave her with a firm, 'I'd rather have dirty feet than a broken ankle.'

In fact the stone steps were immaculately clean and dust-free, although climbing them ahead of Alessandro, as they were only wide enough for one person, was causing her heart to pound erratically. Not because she was so very aware of him behind her, of course. No, it was because there were so many of them, winding upwards in the narrow tower, and the climb was dizzying her and leaving her short of breath.

At last the top was reached—an empty round space with whitewashed walls and a wooden floor, dark with age. One door was set into the curved wall, and Alessandro opened it for her.

Leonora wasn't sure what she had expected. The plain bareness of the tower and its stone steps were such a contrast to the almost over-powering extravagance of the main entrance and the hallway of the *castello*. The hallway that lay beyond this door, though, was surprisingly modern, reminding her of the skilled renovation of Alessandro's apartment. A niche in one of the walls held a piece of abstract sculpture, and the chandelier looked similarly modern. The floor-boards pale and smooth, simple linen curtains were at the window, and the window seat was covered in a matt black fabric with a fine grey and white stripe, creating a classically under-stated look.

A pair of carved double doors opened into a large room in much the same style as the hallway, but Leonora wasn't paying any atten-tion to its décor. Instead she was staring with horror at the enormous bed dominating the room.

'This isn't the only bedroom, is it?' she asked Alessandro.

'If you mean is this the only bedroom in the *castello*, then it is not. If you mean is it the only bedroom here in this suite—then, yes, it is,' he answered her promptly.

Leonora badly wanted to sit down. 'But we can't share a bedroom,' she protested.

The look he gave her was icy with disdain and sharp with impatience. 'We don't have any other option.'

'But there's only one bed.'

'Which is at least six feet wide. And I assure you that even if it were not, I do not have any intention of turning our public relationship as supposed lovers into a private reality. I thought I had already made that much clear to you? Unless, of course, what you fear is that you yourself may be so overcome with lust for me that you—'

'No!' Leonora stopped him hurriedly. 'Of course not.'

'Then there is nothing for you to fear,' he told her with a dismissive shrug. 'I agree that there will be a certain amount of inconvenience, but we are both adults, and I am sure that we are perfectly capable between us of working out a means of not intruding on one another's need for privacy.'

Not trusting herself to say anything, Leonora

walked over to the windows and looked out, startled to discover that all she could see was the sea.

'This tower is built into the original walls,' Alessandro told her. 'It is one of only three that our ancestor left standing when he started his rebuilding programme. It is linked to the main house by a corridor through the doors opposite the windows, whilst the doors on either side of the bed lead respectively to a dressing room and the bathroom. I dare say that our cases will already have been brought up and unpacked.'

'I can't share a room with you,' Leonora insisted as the full recognition of exactly what that was going to mean burst in on her.

It wasn't just a matter of them having to share a bed. They would be sharing a bathroom. She would have to dress and undress in the same room as him. She would have to be there when he dressed and undressed. The fierce kick of excitement with which her body greeted that knowledge was not the reaction she wanted to admit to having.

'You have no choice,' Alessandro told her.

CHAPTER SEVEN

IN THE end it wasn't as bad as she had been dreading. Alessandro disappeared into the hallway with his laptop, whilst she showered in the enormous state-of-the-art bathroom, with its wet room and its huge roll-top bath. He left her the privacy of the dressing room in which to dress, whilst he showered and then dressed in the bedroom, in clothes he had removed from the dressing room beforehand.

Her new hairstyle was surprisingly easy to manage, and so too were the make-up tricks of the trade she had been taught. But what she was *not* able to do was zip her dress all the way up the back. No matter how hard she tried it remained stubbornly a few millimetres from the top—and nor could she fasten the tiny hook and eye at the very top of the zip.

She could, of course, always ask Alessandro to do it for her, but she wasn't going to admit to him that she needed his help with anything. Besides, given what he had already said about her being overcome with lust for him, he might think that she was using some kind of deliberate ploy, pretending that she couldn't fasten her zip. She certainly wasn't going to have him accuse her of that. Anyway, the zip was secure enough, and the dress's slender shoulder straps were holding it in place.

She heard him rap briefly on the door and call out, 'Are you ready?'

Calling back, 'Yes,' she opened the door. Dressed in jeans and a shirt Alessandro had been impressive, but dressed in a dinner suit he was more than impressive. He was... Leonora gulped and swallowed, and willed her heartbeat to resume a more normal rhythm as she went to join him.

The cocktail dress stroked silkily against her skin, sensitising her nerve-endings—or was it Alessandro's presence that was doing that?

When he went to open the door for her the thin plain gold cufflinks gleamed discreetly in the light, and Leonora's heart gave a series of small skipping beats. Had she met a man like Alessandro when she was younger, would she still be a virgin? A man like Alessandro? No, there could not possibly be another. He was unique, a one-off—and besides, she suspected that a man of his sexual experience and expertise would be contemptuous of if not outright repelled by a woman like her.

Hadn't he already said as much, when he had told her that, having kissed her once, he had no desire to do so again? But he *had* kissed her again. For show—as part of the role he had decided they must both play—not for any other reason. What mattered most now was that she didn't give in to her own weakness, and that she didn't allow Alessandro to see or guess that she might be vulnerable to allowing him to win in any kind of contest between them. He had defeated her once by blackmailing her. Her pride would not allow her to acknowledge him as the victor a second time.

They were in a corridor, bare-walled and obviously old, which then opened up into a wider gallery panelled in dark wood and hung with heavily framed portraits.

'This corridor is just short of a quarter of a mile long. My brothers and I used to ride our bikes along here in wet weather,' Alessandro informed her, breaking the silence between them. 'There are no rooms off it, just two sets of stairs—one that goes down to the kitchens and up to what originally were the servants' quarters and the nursery, and another to my father's private apartments. It was one of his rules that we were not allowed to use the gallery in case we disturbed him whilst he was "working"—that being his euphemism for being with his mistress. He didn't spare the rod when any of us were caught transgressing.'

Leonora was appalled. 'My father never hit any of us. He wasn't that kind of man. In fact he would have encouraged us to use a gallery, and would probably have made us race against one another. Dad loves competitive sports, but most of all he loves winners.'

Alessandro frowned as he listened, his anger at himself for telling Leonora something so personal about his childhood vanquished by his reaction to her comment about her father. Maybe he had not physically abused his children, as Alessandro's own father had done, but there were other ways of inflicting pain on the young and vulnerable. Alessandro could see quite plainly that Leonora felt inferior to her brothers, although he knew that she would fiercely deny feeling any such thing were he to suggest it. The very fact that she had gone to such reckless lengths to prove that she could fly not just as well as but better than Leo proved that. It wasn't merely a matter of doing better, though. It was more than that. It was a need to be accepted and valued in a family situation where only the first was valued.

If he were to say as much to her she would reject his assessment, of course, just as he would have done himself if their positions had been reversed. But she could not hide the truth from him. He could see and understand her motivation as clearly as though it had been his own. Because her reaction was so close to what his own would have been? Alessandro's frown deepened. This was the first time he had recognised in someone else the emotions that had so often driven him, and it wasn't a welcome or pleasant discovery.

He didn't want to recognise in Leonora his own vulnerabilities, and he most certainly did not want to accept that the two of them shared something as personal as the same kind of emotional triggers, resulting from their childhoods. Besides, their circumstances were not the same. He was the middle one in a trio of same-sex siblings; she was a girl in between two brothers. Which meant what? That she felt driven to compete with the male sex as a whole as well as to do better than her brothers? Potentially that would make her a woman who saw sex as yet another means of beating her male partner, since men traditionally were seen as the sexual instigators and the victors. She would feel a need to usurp that role. So why hadn't she made any attempt to challenge him sexually?

Alessandro had a keenly analytical brain, and he didn't like problems that did not add up. Right now—irritatingly—the problem that was Leonora Thaxton most definitely did not add up.

Just as Leonora was beginning to think it might

have been a good idea for her to wear a pair of flat shoes for this hike, Alessandro turned towards a pair of double doors that opened up into a vaulted-ceilinged salon filled with dark furniture. They had to weave their way through it to reach another set of doors. The atmosphere of the room felt heavy with disapproval, and Leonora was glad to leave it behind even though the library they were now in felt just as unwelcoming.

Eventually, after traversing two more darkly formal rooms, they emerged onto another corridor—much shorter this time—which in turn brought them to an imposing flight of stairs that led down into the hallway Leonora recognised from their arrival.

Now for the first time—although as far as she could see there was no one below them in the hallway—Alessandro offered her his arm, so that they could descend the stairs together as a couple. Just as she had done before, Leonora noted how even with four-inch heels she was still several inches shorter than Alessandro. How odd it was that along with additional height had come the feeling of being unfamiliarly fragile and feminine. And, even more disconcertingly, the absurd impulse to move closer to Alessandro, tucking herself against him so that their shared descent of the stairs brought her hip into brief contact with his body.

When he felt Leonora moving closer to him Alessandro told himself that the only reason he was allowing her to do so was because their physical closeness would help to convince on-lookers of her total commitment to him. That there were not as yet any onlookers to observe them as he adjusted his grasp on her elbow to keep her close was, he decided, immaterial. Before long there would be, and it was impor-tant that their intimacy came across as natural and second nature.

Once they were down in the hallway Alessandro guided Leonora towards the open double doors she had noticed before, and through them into an elegant salon littered with gilded furniture. Some of it was decorated with Egyptian motifs and some was covered in faded powder-blue silk, patterned with what Leonora guessed must be the family arms in gold thread.

The room was illuminated by two chandeliers, their light thrown back by several pairs of gilded wall mirrors. Several low tables were crammed with small ornaments.

'Some of the decor in these rooms dates from the time of Napoleon, shortly after his victorious campaign in Egypt,' Alessandro informed Leonora. 'The blue silk was specially woven to incorporate the family's arms. It's rumoured that at one time our ancestor had ambitions to marry his eldest son off to Napoleon's sister Pauline. It was perhaps just as well that he didn't succeed.'

As they went through another room, decorated in faded yellow this time, Leonora could hear the hum of conversation coming from the next room. An imposingly liveried footman complete with a powdered wig emerged from the room, carrying an empty tray, and was quickly followed by another. Nervous apprehension bubbled in Leonora's stomach, for all the world as though she were in reality a young woman about to meet the father of the man she loved for the first time.

However, as she held back, Falcon suddenly

came through the door saying easily, 'There you are,' and then she was stepping into the room on Alessandro's arm, whilst Falcon shepherded them through the small throng of guests, many of them members of the older generation, with the men wearing rows of medals and decorations that matched their wives' jewellery for magnificence.

The old Prince was seated in what Leonora suspected was a chair made to support an invalid, although it was plain that Alessandro's father considered it to be more of a throne. His silver hair glinted in the light, and his features were as proudly arrogant as those of his second son. One hand, its knuckles swollen with age, was gripping the silver head of a walking stick. He was a very regal figure indeed, Leonora thought, and then checked that thought as he turned his head to look at her. In place of Alessandro's proud gaze she saw that his father's eyes were small and his gaze spiteful, with a lifetime's worth of self-indulgence and conceit evident in his expression. Her first thought was that he was not worthy of being Alessandro's father—and her second was that she had no right to be thinking such thoughts.

As though a silent order had been given, a pathway to the old Prince had been cleared for them by the other guests, and the room was gripped by a watchful silence. Plainly the hostility that existed between father and son was common knowledge, Leonora recognised.

'So, Alessandro—you are taking a dangerous risk, aren't you? Bringing your friend here? How many times do I need to warn you that a mere second son must always run the risk of being supplanted—in all things—by the first-born? A woman will always look for the best possible father for her children—which is why first-born sons get the pick of the crop, and second-born sons have to make do with what is left or rejected.'

The Prince wasn't just cruel, he was wicked as well, Leonora thought angrily. What a dreadful thing to say to his own son—and in public. He had just implied that Alessandro could never hope to keep the woman he loved if his brother should want her. The Prince wasn't just insulting Alessandro, he was insulting her as well.

Before she could stop herself, Leonora drew herself up proudly and announced firmly, 'Alessandro knows that no one could ever take his place in my life or in my heart.' Leonora could almost feel the concerted indrawn breath of her audience. 'And as for him being a second son—that adds to my love for him instead of detracting from it.'

'Only a fool would believe that. There is no woman alive who would not wish to see her own son succeeding to the family's titles rather than the child of her husband's older brother. Your sex has lied, cheated and killed to claim such a birthright,' the Prince told her coldly.

'Maybe centuries ago, but in these modern times what a mother wants for her child is a loving father and the chance for that child to grow up free of the restrictions imposed on it by family expectation. Alessandro's gifts to his children will be far, far greater than an empty and meaningless title.'

Leonora could feel the wave of astonishment surging round her, and the euphoria she felt at having stepped in to defend Alessandro quickly retreated when she turned to look at him and saw that, far from looking pleased with her, Alessandro was looking at her very grimly indeed.

The Prince hadn't finished.

'Pah!' he exclaimed. 'You may believe that now, but no woman wants a man who stands silent whilst she has to defend him. But then you were always one to run for protection behind a woman's skirts, weren't you, Alessandro? You haven't changed.'

'And neither have you, Father,' Alessandro told him contemptuously. 'However, I have no wish to become involved in an exchange of verbal insults with a sick old man whose life has not much longer to run—much as I dare say you would like to force me to do.'

Without giving his father a chance to say any more, Alessandro gripped Leonora's arm and turned round, immediately introducing her to the middle-aged couple standing behind them. They were a local dignitary and his wife, whom Alessandro engaged in conversation about a restoration project on some civic buildings, the cost of which Leonora learned he was contributing to.

The local dignitary obviously had a high opinion of Alessandro, and Leonora guessed that his sympathy lay with him—although he did not allude to the sharp exchange of words that had just taken place between father and son.

The Prince seemed to be a law unto himself, with no regard for the feelings of others—especially those of his second son. Growing up with such a father must have been hard—far, far harder than her own childhood. Her father might have encouraged rivalry and competition between them, and not been aware of the emotional needs of a teenage girl, but he did love them all. The Prince, on the other hand, did not appear to have any love for any of his sons.

Alessandro excused them both to the local dignitary and his wife, saying that he wanted to introduce Leonora to as many people as possible, but he pulled her into an alcove and stood in front of her, blocking both her escape and the curious looks of anyone else.

'If my father had paid you to humiliate me, you could not have done a better job for him,' he said, quietly and savagely.

Immediately Leonora snapped back, 'I was just trying to defend you, that's all.'

'Defend me?' Her protest seemed to increase his anger rather than lessen it. 'That's my role—not yours. A man defends *himself* and those who depend on him. A woman defends her child. But of course you couldn't resist seizing control, could you? Even though it meant humiliating me—the man, I might remind you, you are supposed to love.'

'You're accusing *me* of seizing control? That's rich, coming from you! And you'd be able to see that for yourself if you weren't so obsessed with proving to your father that being second born doesn't stop you from being a success.'

'I have nothing to prove to anyone, least of all my father. The only opinion and approval that matters to me is my own.'

They glared at one another as they exchanged increasingly furious whispers.

'Rubbish,' Leonora told him. 'If that was the truth you'd never have blackmailed me and brought me here. You know your trouble—'

'I certainly know *yours*,' Alessandro interrupted her. 'You just can't allow a man to be a man because you have to compete with him. In fact you are so obsessed with competing with my sex that you've turned yourself into a sexless mutation of a woman who thinks that men are turned on by an Amazonian intent on fighting their battles for them.'

'That's not true.' Leonora's voice trembled slightly, but deep down inside herself she knew that his unkind words had struck a painful chord.

How often had her brothers teased her that she frightened off their sex? Their teasing had hurt, but she had hidden that from them, not knowing how to change what she had become. It wasn't true, though, that she'd always wanted to compete with men and beat them. Deep down inside she longed for a man she could trust so implicitly that she could let down her guard with him—someone who would understand her and not laugh at her, but instead help her regain her womanhood. But how could she ever trust any man to that extent when she already feared rejection so much?

Alessandro knew he was overreacting, but listening to Leonora defending him had awakened painful memories of his childhood, of both his mother's and later Falcon's attempts to protect him from his father. He hated the memory of his vulnerability and inability to protect himself. It was his job to protect Leonora, not the other way around, but she had not allowed him to do so. Instead she had helped his father to humiliate him.

'Remember why you are here,' Alessandro warned Leonora as he stepped back from her. 'And if you want to defend a member of my sex, think about your brother.'

The room they were in had gradually filled up with new arrivals, and Leonora became separated from Alessandro, who had been appropriated by a stunning-looking woman who had put her arm through his and given Leonora an openly false smile as she had claimed that she promised to take Alessandro over to talk to her husband. There hadn't been any husband anywhere at hand five minutes later, when she had seen them standing close together, the brunette gazing up hungrily into Alessandro's face.

Not that she cared, of course. In fact she was glad to be relieved of his company after the way he had spoken to her. And yet for some reason she could feel a lump of misery forming in her throat, even though she was doing her best to circulate and speak to people. A strangely persistent man had just penned her into a corner and kept on asking her when an official announcement was going to be made. In the end she had escaped by telling him that he would have to ask Alessandro himself.

A passing waiter offered her a fresh drink but she shook her head. She wasn't used to eating so late, and she had gone beyond hunger now to the point where she actually felt slightly sick and dizzy from a mixture of unrequited hunger, misery and tiredness. A discreet glance at her watch told her that it was only just nine o'clock—another hour to go before they would be eating.

Her feet ached in the high heels, and she eased her foot out of one of them, sighing as it fell over. Unable to slip it back on while standing, she reached down to replace the shoe—and then realised to her horror that her movement had caused her zip to slide down. Straightening up, she hugged the now loose top of her dress to her body and tried at the same time to walk backwards towards the wall, wondering what on earth she was going to do. She had no idea where the nearest loo might be, and it was impossible for her to re-zip her dress discreetly. It would need two hands and a good deal of effort—and even then she would not be able to fasten it completely, as she already knew.

Standing frozen with apprehension, her arms folded beneath her breasts, she longed to simply magically disappear. Alessandro would be furious if she showed him up, and she wasn't exactly keen herself on the thought of her dress falling off—especially as all she was wearing underneath it was a pair of nude-coloured briefs.

'Cold?'

Falcon. Leonora gulped and shook her head, and then felt her heart sink even further as one of her shoulder straps fell down.

'That was a very passionate defence you made of Sandro,' Falcon commented with a smile.

'I feel very passionately about him,' Leonora

told him. That much was true, after all. She didn't have to say that the passion she felt was of the angry rather than the sensual variety.

'He's angry with me now. He said that I humiliated him.' Leonora didn't know why she had made the admission, except that there was something about Falcon's quiet demeanour that invited confessions like a magnet.

'He's a very proud man.'

'Yes.'

'Are you sure you aren't cold?'

Once again Leonora shook her head. And then, deciding that Falcon might well be her only chance of escaping from the room without losing both her dignity and her dress, she admitted, 'It's my dress. The zip wasn't fastened properly and now it's come down. I daren't move in case it comes down even more.'

'Ah, I see. Well, in that case—since Alessandro isn't here to do the chivalrous thing and rescue you, perhaps as I am his brother you will allow me to do so for you?'

Where normally she would have felt uncomfortable and embarrassed, instead she actually felt strangely relieved—and very safe. Just as though she and Alessandro actually were an item, and Falcon was a sort of extra brother.

'If you could,' she said gratefully. 'Only I don't know how you can help me without anyone seeing.'

'Easy. I shall just do this,' Falcon told her with another smile, and he reached out and pulled her firmly towards him, so that she was half at right angles to his body, with her shoulder tucked into his chest.

He screened her from the other guests and then reached behind her to ease up the zip with the kind of skill that told her Alessandro's brother was perfectly familiar with the complexities of fastening zips on female clothes. He even managed the hook and eye for her. Leonora gave him a smile of relieved gratitude.

On the other side of the room Alessandro watched Leonora and his brother with mounting fury. He had told her expressly not to flirt with Falcon, and yet that was exactly what she was doing—looking up at him with that doe-eyed look, smiling at him, laughing with him—whilst

Falcon stood far too close to her. Fury—and it was fury, not jealousy, Alessandro assured himself—shot through him, every bit as potent and dangerous as Mount Etna erupting. It spewed rage through him like hot ashes and lava, burning its caustic path inside his head. She was doing it deliberately—she had to be. Well, she'd soon learn that that no one, least of all her, played him for a fool.

CHAPTER EIGHT

'I HOPE you enjoyed flirting with my brother, because it has cost *your* brother his job.'

They were on their way in for the buffet dinner for the house guests, but Alessandro's words had Leonora stopping in her tracks.

'I wasn't flirting with anyone.'

'Liar,' he contradicted her flatly. 'I saw you with my own eyes. And don't think I don't know why you went expressly against my orders. You just *had* to try to make your point, didn't you? But you'll never compete with me and win, Leonora. I'm not that kind of man.'

'No. It wasn't like that at all,' she protested immediately. 'The trouble with you is that you're so obsessed with proving that being a second son doesn't make you second rate that you think that everyone's out to challenge you, even when they aren't.'

Her accusation infuriated Alessandro. He grabbed hold of her arm and almost dragged her into a small empty ante-room, closing the door and then telling her, 'Falcon might flirt with you and allow you to think that he wants you, but I can tell you now that he doesn't. The only reason he would show any interest in you would be out of some misguided belief that he needs to protect me. But I never make the same mistake twice. Once I might have been foolish enough to allow a woman to convince me that she wanted me, when all she really wanted was to use me as a stepping stone to get to Falcon, and everything that marrying him would have given her. But the speed with which she transferred her affections from me to Falcon taught me a lesson I haven't forgotten.'

And what a painful lesson that would have been for him, Leonora recognised, given his pride and the cruelty with which his father rein-forced his second-son status.

'Do you still love her?'

The words were out before she could stop herself, and she wasn't surprised when she saw a look of grim disbelief that she should ask such a personal question darkening his eyes.

'I never loved her,' he told her flatly. 'But I swore that I'd never allow myself to be publicly humiliated again by a woman transferring her affections from me to someone else—especially not to Falcon, however well-meaning his intentions. Which is why—'

'Why you blackmailed me into coming here with you.'

'Which is why your behaviour has just cost your brother his job,' Alessandro repeated.

'But I wasn't flirting with Falcon. You can ask him, if you like.'

'I don't need to ask him. I have eyes, and I could see what was going on.'

'No, you couldn't. Because what was "going on", as you call it, was that my zip had come down because I hadn't been able to fasten it properly. Falcon was zipping it up again for me.'

There was a ring of truth in her voice that forced Alessandro to listen.

'If that's true then why didn't you ask *me* to fasten it for you before we left our room?'

Good question. Leonora weighed up the consequences of telling the truth or trying to bluff her way out with a fabrication. She'd never been a good liar, so she took a deep breath and told him honestly, 'I didn't want you to think I was trying to…'

'To what?' Alessandro pressed impatiently.

Leonora tilted her chin and told him defensively, 'I didn't want you thinking that I was trying to…well, come on to you.'

Her statement was too ridiculous not to be the truth, Alessandro decided.

'And you have the gall to accuse *me* of being paranoid?' he said in disbelief, reaching for the door to open it as he added, 'Very well, I'll accept your explanation—on this occasion.'

'That's big of you,' Leonora muttered to herself as he held the door open for her.

She didn't realise that Alessandro had heard her until he agreed coldly, 'Yes, it is. And there'd better not be any more similar errors of judgement on your part, because I certainly shan't be as lenient a second time.'

Much as she was tempted to challenge his

arrogant attitude, Leonora decided against it. Not whilst he was holding over her the power to hurt her brother.

The evening was drawing to a close, and as Leonora fought to suppress her yawns Alessandro leaned towards her and said quietly, 'You're tired. You may as well go up to the room. I'll follow you later.'

His apparent consideration for her now, contrasted with his attitude towards her earlier, caught her off guard, and touched her emotions in a way she didn't want. Quickly she nodded her head, accepting his discreet hint that he was offering her the chance to get ready for bed in privacy.

As she stood up, Falcon, who had been engaged in conversation with someone seated further down the table, pushed his own chair back and came over to say, 'You are going to bed? Then I shall say goodnight.'

Leonora began to smile politely, but to her shock Falcon placed his hands on her arms and kissed her, first on one cheek and then the other.

He was Sicilian, of course. And there had been

nothing in the least bit sensual or sexual about his embrace. He did, after all, think that she and Alessandro were a couple. Still, she felt rather self-conscious, turning away from him as soon as he had released her, only to find that Alessandro had also stood up and was now standing in front of her. As she made to sidestep him he stopped her, taking hold of her hand and drawing her towards him, then bending his head.

By the time she realised that he was going to kiss her it was too late to do anything to try to stop him. His mouth was on hers, his arm around her, her own lips softening into mute obedience at the command of his. A swift glance upwards revealed the glint of his eyes between the dark frame of his lashes. Mesmerised and helpless, she felt the aftershock of her own response to him, swiftly pulling back from him, her face on fire.

It was a relief to get away and follow the footman who had been summoned to escort her back to the tower suite.

As they left the salon behind she acknowledged that, to her own surprise, she had actually enjoyed some parts of the evening. She had met some fascinating people, and had learned a great deal about the lives of Alessandro and his brothers as young boys. Everyone had mentioned how sad it had been for them to lose their mother, and there had even been discreet and not so discreet references to their father's second marriage to his mistress, and his preference for the son he had with her over his sons by his first wife. She had learned too how unpopular Antonio had been and how many people thought that his death at the wheel of his sports car had removed a very unpleasant character from their lives. Alessandro himself had been spoken of with both admiration and respect for all that he had achieved.

When they reached the door to the tower suite the footman made a small half-bow to her, indicating that he was about to depart, and Leonora thanked him before opening the door and letting herself into the suite.

Her feet ached from her high-heeled shoes, and it was a relief to take them off. She'd have loved to soak in a long bath, but she wasn't sure how much time she would have before

Alessandro arrived. Luckily she was able to unfasten the hook and eye on her dress and then the zip. After stepping out of it in the dressing room she hung it up and padded barefoot, wearing only her briefs, through the bedroom in which the bed had been turned down, averting her gaze from its intimacy and hurrying into the bathroom.

Alessandro frowned as he watched Falcon, who was seated several feet away from him, deep in conversation with one of the guests. The feeling of acute and immediate male possessiveness he had experienced when Falcon had kissed Leonora goodnight hadn't entirely subsided. Not that Leonora really meant anything to him, of course. No? Then why had he felt it so necessary to reinforce the fact that she was his? No reason. It had simply been a gut reaction, that was all. Impatiently he pushed back his chair, bidding those around him goodnight.

Removing her underwear, Leonora stepped into the glass-sided wet-room-style shower and turned on the water. The sensation of the powerful spray against her skin felt wonderful, and the heat of the water released the scent of the shower gel she'd found waiting for her in a basket of bathroom necessities.

She was so tired she'd be asleep the minute her head touched the pillow, Leonora decided thankfully, and she certainly had no fears that Alessandro would try to take advantage of the situation, despite the way he had kissed her downstairs in the salon. That had just been for show.

She reached out and turned off the water. She was about to step out of the shower when she saw it.

It was the most enormous spider she had ever seen, and it was crouching right in front of her exit from the shower. The only way she could get past it would be to step over it. A sick shudder ripped through her. She was terrified of spiders, always had been. Her brothers, of course, had been delighted to discover that their sister could be terrorised by creatures they were quite happy to pick up, and had teased her dreadfully with them until the day she had fainted when Leo had tried to put one down the back of her T-shirt.

What would it do? Would it come into the shower?

She started to shake, the blood leaving her face. She dared not take her gaze off it in case it moved. It was staring back at her. She was sure it was. Her stomach churned. She was a quivering mass of total terror. She knew that her fear was irrational, but knowing it didn't help. Nothing had ever helped.

The spider lifted one leg—and then another. A petrified scream bubbled in her throat, but her throat muscles were too stiff with terror to let it escape. Her whole body was now rigid, her heart thundering into her chest wall so hard and so fast that it was making her feel dizzy. But she mustn't faint, because then it might run all over her. A deep shudder broke her rigidity.

Alessandro opened the bedroom door, removing his dinner jacket as he closed it. All the lights were on but there was no sign of Leonora. He had expected that she would be in bed by now. He unfastened his bow tie and opened the top buttons of his dress shirt.

Formal occasions and formal clothes were not his favourite things. Removing the cufflinks from his cuffs, he walked towards the dressing room. The door was open, and there was no sign of Leonora inside it, which meant that she must be in the bathroom.

He walked towards the half-open door, rapping on it warningly before calling out, 'Leonora?'

Alessandro. Relief bubbled in Leonora's throat, and her gaze immediately went to the door—only to return swiftly to the spider. It had moved. It was coming into the shower.

Alessandro heard her scream and thrust open the bathroom door. She was huddled in a corner of the shower, naked and white-faced, one hand against her breasts, the other covering her sex, her eyes dark with terror.

'What is it?' Alessandro demanded, perplexed.

Leonora removed her hand from her breasts, every bit as softly full as he had imagined, with peach tip-tilted nipples, hard now, presumably from the cold, since he could see goosebumps on her arms. Between the fingers of her other splayed hand he could see the soft feathery curls of the hair covering her sex, and her modesty was somehow more erotic and tantalising than if she had been standing there naked. Her body had a lushness he hadn't expected, and his own was responding to it.

'It's a spider.' Her voice was thin with fear, and her body was shuddering as she looked at him, and then looked down again at the limestone floor, her breath catching in a terrified gasp as she cowered against the back of the shower. 'It's moving. Oh, please…no…'

Alessandro had never thought of himself as a potential hero—he was too cynical—but something about her obvious terror had him reacting as swiftly as any would-be James Bond. He reached for a towel, which he dropped over the spider, and then speedily lifted Leonora bodily from the shower, to hold her tightly as she shuddered convulsively in his arms in between sobs.

Grabbing another larger towel, he carried her into the bedroom and then put her down, wrapping the towel round her before heading back to the bathroom. He was just about to remove the towel from the trapped spider when he heard Leonora calling out shakily.

'Please don't kill it. It isn't its fault that I'm terrified of it.'

A woman who hated spiders and yet who wouldn't allow one to be despatched? She really was a one of a kind, he reflected as he scooped up the spider and very gently tipped it from his hand out of the bathroom window, and then closed the window.

Wrapped in her towel, but still shivering slightly with reaction, Leonora looked anxiously at Alessandro when he came back into the bedroom.

'What did you do with it?'

'Don't worry, it's quite safe and in one piece, with all its legs intact. I put it out of the window.'

'You must think I'm a total idiot.'

'You're a woman,' he told her. 'You're allowed to be—'

'An idiot?' she challenged him.

'Afraid of spiders,' he corrected her.

'Thanks for...for what you did. My brothers would have laughed.'

She looked up at him. Now that the spider had been removed and her terror had eased, she was beginning to feel acutely self-conscious. She had been naked in the shower, after all, and he had picked her up and…

'Your shirt's all wet now.' Her voice had gone husky, and her gaze was fastened on his torso, her heart thudding in a primitive beat that her body recognised and her mind shied away from in shock.

Alessandro shrugged. Wrapped in a towel, her hair tousled and her lips still trembling slightly from shock, she looked far too enticing. He watched as she touched the tip of her tongue to her lips, her gaze still concentrated on his body. Immediately he felt his own banked-down desire kick into fierce life as it recognised the subtle message she was giving him. He might have told himself that there must not be any intimacy between them, but that had been before he had seen her in Falcon's embrace and known that the only male arms he was prepared to tolerate seeing wrapped around her were his own.

'Then perhaps I'd better take it off. Or, even better, why don't you take it off for me?'

Leonora exhaled on an unsteady breath of intense longing. She didn't know how she had got to this point, but now that she was here she knew that she didn't want to turn back.

'I'm not very good at this kind of thing,' she warned him.

Alessandro looked at her.

'Liar,' he told her softly as he went to her. 'My body says that you are very good at it indeed.'

He was lifting her bodily out of the chair in which he had placed her when he had rescued her from the shower, only this time without the towel. He had pushed it aside, his hands warm and firm on her bare skin, his confidence putting to flight her own untutored hesitancy, compelling her body to recognise in his touch his right of possession.

As he carried her over to the bed she put one arm around his neck, her hand resting against his nape whilst the other instinctively slid inside his open shirt. His chest felt warm and hard, the sensation of muscle packed tight beneath male flesh causing the anticipation already curling through her belly to intensify into a low-lying persistent ache of need. She could feel that need burning, spreading through her, swelling her breasts and tightening her nipples. The fingers of the hand resting against his nape slid into the thick darkness of Alessandro's hair as she looked up at his mouth, her lips parting breathlessly. All her senses seemed to be intensified, her sensual awareness heightened, the mere smell of his skin an aphrodisiac so powerful that it made her weak with longing.

Just the way Leonora was looking at him was having a similar effect to raw spirit taken on a battle-hardened empty stomach, Alessandro recognised, filling him with a surge of primitive testosterone-fuelled male energy far too powerful and all-consuming to be contained by any barriers. Like Mount Etna at its most dangerous, it defied and mocked the frailty of a mere man's attempt to suppress it.

He had reached the bed, but instead of placing Leonora on it he continued to hold her, sitting down on the edge of the bed with her in his arms whilst he accepted the offering of her parted lips, his tongue thrusting deeply and fiercely into the hot, wild intimacy of her kiss, his free hand going to her breast to savour the erotic pleasure of the contrast between the globe's full softness and the tight, hard demand of her swollen nipple.

A wild shudder ripped through Leonora's body, arching her upwards in a mute appeal that begged for more, and she was answered by a thick groan of male enjoyment from Alessandro as he responded to her need, continuing to kiss her whilst he brought her flesh to helpless surrender with the skilled touch of his fingers against her eager nipple.

Just when his hand had left her breast to cover her sex with an immediacy that matched perfectly her own desire she had no idea. All she did know was that—blissfully—its weight against the mound of flesh within which an increasingly frantic longing pulsed brought her a momentary relief that was quickly replaced by an even more intense desire.

Breaking their kiss to look down at Leonora's naked body, Alessandro felt his being gripped with urgency. Her nipples demanded the servitude of his lips. The sensual relaxation of her thighs into her own desire invited the probe of his thumb against the top of the sweetly closed outer lips to her sex, into the liquid heat they enclosed.

Leonora moaned—a long, slow, sweet sound of female pleasure rising from deep within her, mirroring the crescendo of pleasure to which she was being brought by the skilled movement of Alessandro's touch against her clitoris. She wanted both to move with it and hold that pleasure to her, and at the same time she wanted to escape its dominance, fearing that it would overwhelm her. Her body had become an alien, sweetly tormented instrument that responded only to Alessandro's command.

Deep down inside herself she could feel an ache of yearning that could only be satisfied by the shared possession of their flesh, by the feel of him deep within her, the feel of her flesh enclosing him and holding him. A surge of dizzying joy burst through her. At last it was over. Soon she would be the woman she had secretly longed to be for so long—complete, fulfilled, with ownership of the knowledge of her own sexuality and all its secrets given to her by

Alessandro in exchange for her unwanted, soon-to-be cast off burden of virginity.

Leonora tensed in the midst of her lyrical pre-celebration, cold truth shadowing her joy. She couldn't let Alessandro find out that she was still a virgin. It would be the ultimate humiliation. And he would find out if she didn't stop him soon.

Leonora was pushing him away, retreating from him, struggling to sit up—rejecting him, Alessandro recognised. Swiftly he released her, his pride immediately reacting to her recoil from his touch.

'You said that...that this wouldn't happen,' Leonora reminded him. The ache of her body deprived of his touch was so strong that she could hardly bear it. It set all her nerve-endings jangling against the low dragging weight of her unsatisfied desire.

Alessandro got up and strode over to the chair, picking up the towel they had left there, tossing it over to her, keeping his back towards her whilst Leonora wrapped it clumsily around herself. Leonora's accusation stung. He *had* said he wouldn't touch her—but that had been before.

Before what? Before he had seen Falcon looking at her? Before he had walked into the bathroom and felt that surge of arousal that had obliterated everything else?

'I'm a man,' he told Leonora with a dismissive shrug, once he had got his emotions and the fierce urgency of his still-aching need for her under control and was able to turn round and look at her. 'You offered yourself to me, so I responded.'

'I was frightened because of the spider,' Leonora defended herself.

The look Alessandro was giving her burned though her fragile defences.

'It was not in fear that you arched beneath my touch, offering yourself to me in all the ways that a sexually aroused woman offers herself to a man, begging for his touch and his possession. If I wished to do so I could show you all over again just how you responded to me. *If* I wished to do so. But I do not.'

His words shamed and scorched her. Leonora wanted to deny them, but how could she? She *had* responded to him. But that had only been because in Alessandro's arms and beneath his touch her secret fantasy of how her imaginary perfect lover would be had come physically and overpoweringly to life. *That* was the reason she had responded to Alessandro as passionately as she had, not because she had wanted Alessandro himself. She could not and must not do that. It was far too risky to let herself want the real man, because then she might— She might what? Fall in love with him and want him for life? Fall in love with Alessandro? How ridiculous—and how very, very fatally dangerous.

He was being ungallant, Alessandro knew, saying things he would normally never have dreamed of saying to a woman, no matter how sexually frustrated he might have felt. But there was something about Leonora that drove him beyond the boundaries of his own rules—something that brought out an emotional passion that infuriated him every bit as much as she did. Neither of those things could be brought within his control, and both of them challenged and taunted him, driving him to want to stamp his possession and his superiority on them, even whilst they remained outside his grasp. Together,

Leonora and his passion for her took him to a place he had thought he had conquered a long time ago, a place in which the supposedly cold ashes of his youthful need to prove himself were suddenly glowing dangerously hot.

Was he really so little in control of himself? So little of a man that a woman's rejection could unleash such a compulsive need to show her that he could make her want him above and beyond all other men? And why *this* woman?

Alessandro was in the bathroom, giving Leonora an opportunity to slip on the silky nightdress that had been part of the new wardrobe she had been supplied with, before getting into the enormous bed and lying as close as she could to its edge.

Alessandro had been right to accuse her of wanting him. She had. She still did. But, as shaming as that accusation had been, it was nothing to the shame she would have experienced had she not stopped him and he had discovered the truth. She had heard her brothers joking about 'ancient' virgins and the horror of accidentally finding one in one's bed. Modern men wanted sexual partners who were accomplished lovers—polished, sophisticated women who were informed and entertaining in bed as well as out of it. She, on the other hand, had felt like a raw novice in Alessandro's arms, giddy with excitement at the thought of the pleasures in store and yet at the same time too overwhelmed by her own excitement to know how to harness it properly.

She had felt like pulling off his shirt and exploring every bit of his torso with her hands as well as smothering it with kisses, when a more knowing woman would probably have aroused him with just one single touch. Alessandro would be a connoisseur of sensuality and all its many pleasures, she suspected, and likely to have nothing but disdain for her inexperienced attempts to show her desire for him.

As he stood under the lash of the shower, waiting for his desire to subside, Alessandro cursed himself. Why had he allowed himself to touch Leonora in the first place? And, having done so, why was he now unable to subdue and dismiss the physical ache for her that was gripping him? She was just a woman, and he never, *ever* allowed any woman to matter so much to him that he could not stop wanting her—much less have that wanting bringing him to the point he was at now.

It was because she had rejected him, that was all. Because she had rejected him here in his childhood home, where the memories of so many other rejections whipped his spirit and his emotions raw of their usual protection.

Why had she changed her mind? She had wanted him. What was she hoping to gain? Did she imagine that by withholding herself from him she could make him want her more—to the point where she was the one controlling him through his desire for her?

Everything that life had taught him to be in order to protect himself burned into life, fiercely repudiating the thought. *He* was the only who controlled his own desires. There never had been and there never would be a woman—any woman—who had the power to make him want her against his will, either physically or emotionally. If Leonora wanted to enter into a competition to see which of them had the most control over their sexuality then he was more than prepared to do so—and to win. And he *would* win. He had to do so. His pride demanded that he did.

Because a small part of him feared that he was not as well defended against her ability to arouse him as he would have liked? Defensive pride held his muscles rigid. He would not and could not tolerate allowing himself to admit that he might want her more than she wanted him. He didn't. And he would prove that to himself before the weekend was over.

Alessandro reached for the tap and turned it to cold, his body tensing as much under the pressure of his thoughts as against the icy blast that shocked it.

CHAPTER NINE

LEONORA woke up abruptly in the darkness. A dull, heavy ache was pressing down on her womb, a sense of emptiness and unsatisfied need. Somehow or other she must have rolled over in her sleep—and not once but at least a couple of times, given the width of the bed, because now, instead of lying on its edge, she was much further over, towards Alessandro's side. She knew that because she was lying facing him, and could see the curve of his naked shoulder where the bedclothes had slipped away. If she were to roll over again she could almost lie curled up against his back…

Resolutely she made herself turn away from him and inch her way back to her own side of the bed. Once there she looked at the luminous face of her watch, which she'd left on the beside table.

Just gone half past two. The room was still and silent, the only movement coming from the curtain. Leonora's heart jumped. Was the window open? If it was then the spider would be able to get back in.

Instantly she was imagining it clambering through the window, dropping down onto the floor, and then making its way towards the bed. Beneath the bedclothes her toes twitched, and apprehension slithered down her spine. She wanted to get up and check the window, to put her mind at rest, but she was too afraid to do so. She tried to think of something else, but the only 'something else' she could think about was how much she wished that things could have been different earlier on in the evening.

What she meant, of course, was how much she wished that *she* could have been different. That she could have been the kind of woman who had the confidence to enjoy the sensual pleasure of being in Alessandro's arms instead of having to remind herself of the reason why she could not allow things to reach their natural conclusion. If she had been then right now she would probably be sleeping safely in his arms, her body replete with the satisfaction of their lovemaking, instead of lying here alone, still aching for him, terrified that the spider might return and miserably aware of how angry she had made him.

She should have brought things to a halt before they had got as far as they had, she admitted, but she had been caught off guard by the intensity of her own response to him. Because she had never allowed herself to be in such a situation before. And because he was, after all, a very, very attractive and sensually powerful man—no woman worthy of the name could fail to be aroused by a man like Alessandro. And she *was* a woman—very much a woman as far as her newly discovered sensual needs went. Even if she hadn't realised that before.

How much she wished now that she had lived her life differently and gained the experience that would have made it easy and natural for her to respond fully to Alessandro in the way she had wanted to. How wonderful it would have been in the future to look back on this time and know that she had lived it to the fullest extent. She had started out resenting Alessandro and everything she believed he stood for, her resentment springing originally from his refusal even to consider employing her. But, having learned what she had about him and his childhood, now knowing that they were both middle children, she felt as though there was a special private bond between them—even though Alessandro himself wasn't aware of it.

A rustle from the curtain jolted her back to her original fear, making her cry out in panic.

Alessandro woke up immediately, automatically sitting up to switch on his bedside light. Its warm glow illuminated the bed, and Leonora's fear-tensed face.

'Is the window open, do you think?' she asked. 'Only if it is the spider might get back in.'

She had bruised his pride earlier, and would certainly have to be punished for that—but not by his making use of her very real fear, Alessandro decided grimly. He would never allow himself to descend to that level, no matter what other people might choose to do. He might feel angrily sure that a combination of her competitive nature and the fact that he had refused to employ her had led to her seizing the opportunity he had accidentally given her to prove that she could best him, but that did not mean he could now allow himself to use her fear against her.

Alessandro had witnessed his father using those kind of underhand tactics too often to want to use them himself. Besides, a victory based on another person's weakness rather than his own strength was no victory at all to Alessandro. No, when she admitted in his arms that she wanted him so much that nothing else mattered it would be because she *did* want to be in his arms, not because fear had driven here there for protection. His father would have called him a fool, no doubt, deriding him as he had done so often when he had been growing up, but his father's opinion of him no longer mattered. He had grown beyond that, and it was now his own moral estimation of himself that was the yardstick by which he measured himself as a man.

Which was why he was putting aside his earlier anger to offer calmly, 'Would you like me to check the window?'

'Would you?' Hope and disbelief mingled in her voice in equal measure. It was an unfamiliar and very fragile feeling to know that a man—especially a man like Alessandro—was willing to do something brave on her behalf. But then during the short time they had spent together she had already experienced more than one unfamiliar feeling with regard to Alessandro.

He was being very generous, given what had happened earlier, and through her fear Leonora felt a renewed stab of guilt for the way she had behaved. She felt so confused and unsure of herself, all too conscious that somehow she had allowed herself to stray into territory she didn't know and where she felt very vulnerable.

It had simply never occurred to her that she would be so attracted to Alessandro, or so helplessly unable to resist the tug of that attraction. The Alessandro Leopardi she had built up inside her head from what Leo had told her about him and, more importantly, from what she had decided he must be like after he had repeatedly rejected her job applications, refusing to acknowledge how well qualified she was to work for him, bore no resemblance to the man who had held her in his arms earlier or the man she was with now.

She tried and failed to imagine either her father or her brothers making the kind of offer that Alessandro had made just now with regard to her arachnophobia. They loved her—of course they did. But their father's robust, competition-focused parenting had affected them all—as Leonora had come to recognise once she had gone out into the wider world to earn her own living. Watching the fathers of her pupils, it had become obvious to her that many of them treated their young daughters very differently from the way they dealt with their young sons.

It was, of course, to her father's credit that he had insisted on treating all of them absolutely equally—he had done his best for them, and it couldn't have been easy losing their mother when they had been so young. They had all suffered. How could they not have? But Leonora suspected that her loss had been the greater. Without a female role model to guide her and teach her how to grow into her femininity she had felt so sad, and even a little envious of the way other fathers parented their little girls. Leonora had come to recognise, as she had watched small girls flirting outrageously with their fathers, that they were being gently taught the appropriate ways of using their feminine gifts in a way that she never had.

It was true that she had learned to moderate the straightforward and outspoken directness her father had taught them all, and it was true that doing so had made her feel more comfortable within herself. But when it came to flirting she felt as clumsy as a would-be juggler, trying to put on an act and having everything come crashing down all around her instead of keeping every-thing spinning effortlessly in the air. And that sent her straight back to the defensive habit of playing the brash tomboy, and watching men recoil from her.

Watching her, and seeing the shadows chasing one another through her eyes, Alessandro dis-covered that he wanted to know what was causing them. Uniquely, in his experience with her sex, she said very little about herself. He knew the basics, of course—he should, given the number of times she had submitted job applications to him—but even in the section allowed for personal comments about aspirations and hopes her words had been blunt, sometimes to the point of aggression, and had focused only on her fierce professional desire. And yet earlier tonight in his arms her response to him had been intense; her passion had meshed with his own desire instead of competing with it.

She had not, as he might have expected her to do, tried to control their intimacy. Instead—surprisingly, given what he knew about her—she had waited for him to take the lead. Why? Because she'd believed she would have a better chance of getting her own way later if she did? She was going to be disappointed if she thought he would change his mind and give her a job. Yes, she was well qualified—far better than many of his pilots—but her presence amongst them would cause trouble.

Had she been plainer in looks or less plain in opinion he might have been tempted to break his own rule, simply because of her qualifications, but it was obvious to him that she would create chaos amongst his existing pilots. There would be those who would champion her because of her looks and those who would oppose her because of the competitive streak in her nature which came across so clearly in her applications. Either way it would have led to the kind of fall-out that wasn't just divisive but was also, in his opinion, potentially dangerous. When he hired a pilot he needed him to be totally focused on his work. Not focused on a woman like Leonora.

If she could get under *his* skin, when he prided himself on being immune to any kind of female manipulation, then what chance did his pilots have?

But what he wanted to know even more was why she was so intent on securing a job with his airline, and if he was right to suspect that, having failed to do so via her professional pilot's skills, she was now attempting to do it via a very different set of skills. What would happen if he *did* try to dig a bit deeper?

There was only one way to find out, Alessandro told himself as he thrust back the bedclothes and stood up. Normally he slept completely naked, but tonight after his shower he'd put on fresh underwear—not that he had imagined for one minute that he would be called upon to take on anti-spider-invasion duties, he thought humorously.

He started to make his way towards the window, stopping at Leonora's side of the bed to say, in a deliberately light voice, 'You never mentioned your arachnophobia on your many CVs, as far as I can remember.'

'My brothers have teased me so much all my life about it that I've developed a second phobia about admitting it to anyone.' Leonora tried to joke back as she sat up in the bed, drawing up her knees protectively, just in case the spider was about, but it was hard to concentrate on exchanging light-hearted banter when Alessandro was standing so close to her wearing so little.

His body was superbly muscled, tapering downwards from his shoulders in an athletic male V shape. His chest was lightly covered with the dark hair she had already seen, which she could now see also arrowed downwards across his flat belly to disappear beneath the top of his underwear. Underwear which, though perfectly respectable, nevertheless revealed just how very much of a man he was. Her eyes rounded slightly and she tried to drag her gaze away. He was *magnificently* male, she thought, gulping back a treacherous sigh of longing. What would it be like to be the kind of woman who felt confident enough to touch him there intimately—to hold him and know him? Her face burned hot at the danger of her own out-of-control thoughts. She prayed that he hadn't noticed she hadn't been able to help looking at him.

Alessandro had noticed, but he was more concerned about controlling his body's reaction to her look than he was about the look itself. How could one look from a woman he had every reason to suspect was trying to manipulate him arouse him so immediately when he normally had no difficulty whatsoever in resisting women coming on to him far more strongly?

As he turned away from her towards the window, he reminded himself of what he was supposed to be doing and said, 'I know that most boys go through a stage when it affords them a huge amount of pleasure to tease girls, but I should have thought that your parents—especially your mother—would have intervened once they realised you had a very real phobia.'

'Our mother died when I was eight. She was killed by a speeding car when she was on her way to collect us all from school. Dad thought the best way for me to get over my fear was to be embarrassed into not being afraid. He always encouraged us to be competitive with one another, and I think he thought that if the boys teased me—especially Piers, because he's the eldest—then I'd do anything to prove that I wasn't afraid. I did try.' She gave a small defeated shrug of her shoulders. 'I hated conceding defeat and being called a cry-baby. But I just could not stop being afraid.'

Alessandro was glad that he had his back to her—and not just because her earlier visual focus on his sex had aroused him. Now he had something else he didn't want her to see for his own protection. Pity and anger filled him in a fierce surge of unexpected and unwanted emotion. He had to bite back on an instinctive criticism of her father for not handling things better. Even if she herself was not aware of how much she was giving away, he had heard in her voice a defensive awareness that she knew she had been let down, but equally he knew that she would defend her father and her brothers against anyone's criticism.

'It must have been hard for you, growing up without your mother,' he commented, when he had control of himself.

'No harder than it was for my brothers, or than it must have been for you and your brothers,' Leonora responded instantly.

They looked at one another. How well he understood what she was feeling, Alessandro recognised. For reasons he didn't want to analyse too closely, he couldn't bring himself to push her any harder. Not because she aroused any kind of tender feelings within him, he assured himself. No, it was because he believed he owed it to himself not to take an unfair advantage of her when she was so obviously vulnerable. He had a far too clear mental image of her as a girl, all sharp-angled pre-pubescent limbs, and with the defensive competitiveness that would have come from the parenting she had described—a girl growing up in a male environment without her mother.

Grimly Alessandro forced it away. That wasn't how he wanted to think of her. After all, no doubt at some stage she would have learned to twist her father round her little finger, and her brothers too. And yet he couldn't quite banish his awareness of how difficult her childhood must have been. Just like his own? No. They were two very different people with nothing in common. Nothing? So they were both second children—motherless second children. That meant nothing. Nothing at all.

He pulled back the curtain to check the window, which was slightly open. He closed it firmly and then checked the wall and the floor around it, before turning to tell Leonora, 'It's closed now, and I can't see any sign of an intruder.'

Leonora nodded her head, and let her breath escape on a leaky sigh of relief.

'Thank you. I know that you must think me foolish, even though you haven't said so.'

'Foolish for being afraid of spiders—no. But foolishly reckless in other ways, perhaps yes.'

That was as close as he was going to get to warning her that he had his suspicions about her. If she had any sense she would immediately abandon any attempts she might be thinking of making to start a battle between them that she was not going to win. He would never, ever let anyone manipulate him into letting them win—at anything. And she was no exception, shared family position or not.

Foolishly reckless in other ways? What exactly did he mean by that? Leonora didn't know, but she did know that he wasn't paying her a compliment. The tough façade Leonora usually presented to the world should have her challenging him and arguing with him, whilst affecting not to care what he thought, but the private inner Leonora was acutely sensitive to his criticism, and unwilling to risk further hurt by asking for an explanation of it.

Alessandro dropped the curtain and was just about to head back to the bed when, without intending to do any such thing, he stopped and said, 'I can't see any sign of your friend, but if it would make you feel more comfortable I'm quite prepared to swap sides of the bed with you and sleep on your side, seeing as it is closer to the window.'

What on earth had made him make *that* offer? He shouldn't be pandering to her fears. She'd think that she had some kind of hold on him, that he wanted to please her, and that wasn't the case at all.

Astonishment and gratitude had Leonora staring at him, unable to conceal how she felt. She wasn't used to being treated like this, and she certainly hadn't expected to be treated in such a way by Alessandro.

'Would you?' She couldn't conceal her wonderment. 'That would be really kind.'

She was overdoing the wide-eyed 'you are wonderful' stuff so much that if he could have done he would have withdrawn his offer, Alessandro decided. Instead he simply shrugged and told her brusquely, 'Hardly that. I'd simply like to get some sleep.'

Instantly the light died from Leonora's eyes, to be replaced with self-conscious chagrin. Of *course* he wasn't doing it for her—and of *course* he wanted to get some sleep. She didn't trust herself to apologise. She knew he'd be able to tell from her voice how mortified she felt. Instead she moved over to his side of the bed and then tensed, immediately aware of how the scent of his skin clung to the place where he had been lying. Surely if her fear of the spider didn't keep her awake then having to sleep here, lying in Alessandro's body warmth and scent, was bound to do so.

Deliberately she lay with her back towards Alessandro, but of course that didn't stop her from knowing the minute he got into the bed from the dip in the mattress. Closing her eyes, she fought not to be conscious of him—which, oddly, was even harder now than it had been earlier. Perhaps because the verbal intimacy they had shared had in its own way made her feel every bit as vulnerable as the sexual intimacy between them earlier?

She felt the bed dip again. He was moving towards her. Was he going to carry out the threat he had made earlier, about proving to her that she wanted him? Breathless anticipation seized her, obliterating the anxiety she knew she should feel. He was right next to her. She could feel the heat from his body. In fact she could feel his body too, where his leg touched her own. A shower of lava-hot longing spilled through her.

He reached round her, his head above her own as he lifted his hand—to turn her to him? Molten desire stirred the heavy arousal in her lower body, and instinctively she started to turn towards him. Only to hear him say, 'You may want to sleep with the light on, the better to spy on your friend, but I'm afraid I do not.' He reached up and switched off the bedside light she had forgotten was on, and then moved away from her.

It could have been worse, she reassured herself after he had returned to his own side of the bed. He could have realised how she was feeling—or, even worse again, she could actually have turned to him and reached out for him. How humiliating *that* would have been. At least this way all she had to contend with was the ache of her desire, not the ache of a bruised heart. A bruised heart? How could Alessandro bruise her heart? He didn't mean anything to her. Did he? No, of course he didn't.

But lying beneath him as he'd reached over her

to switch off the light had filled Leonora with the most potent surge of longing that just would not go away. All she could think about was what it would be like not just to share the sensual intimacy of sex with him, but also to feel the tender warmth of his arms and the security of his protection. What was the matter with her? Such thoughts were inappropriate and unwanted—and what was worse they were also dangerous and painful.

What the hell was the matter with him? Alessandro asked himself angrily as he lay staring into the darkness, fighting down his need to cross the distance that separated him from Leonora. No matter how much he hated having to admit it, he ached to take her in his arms and caress her back to the responsive, eager woman he had held earlier in the evening.

It was an intensity that was wholly unfamiliar to him. He wasn't some callow youth. The fact that he was sharing a bed with Leonora should not have been a signal to his body to hunger for her. He'd been too long without sex—that was his problem. There was nothing personal in the potent mix of emotional and physical need that was now gripping him. He'd spent too much time working and not enough time playing, and he'd let her get under his skin and arouse a dangerous curiosity about her—something he would normally never have allowed to happen. Something that would *not* have happened if he hadn't been obliged by family duty to come here to the *castello* in the first place.

Returning to his childhood home had brought back too many unwanted memories. That was how Leonora had been able to arouse his sympathy. Listening to her talk about her childhood had taken him far too close to the misery of his own. At least her father had loved her in his own way—unlike his father, who had never loved him and had said so. Nothing had changed there. His father's hostility towards him was still there, underpinned by angry contempt. With his own sons he would behave very differently, Alessandro thought. They would all be loved equally and individually, each one of them uniquely precious to him and valued by him, and so would his daughters.

Sons and daughters? What on earth was he thinking? He'd already decided that it was unlikely that he would be a father, since he doubted that he'd ever meet a woman he could trust enough to make the kind of commitment that would lead to them having children. Perhaps it was old-fashioned of him, but he'd want his children to be born into a marriage that would last a lifetime—for their sakes more than for his own. He liked beautiful women, and felt no shame in his preference, but it seemed to him that modern women treated their beauty as a commodity they could sell to the highest bidder for their own advantage, going from marriage to marriage and collecting an impressive portfolio of divorce settlements on the way—just as Sofia had done.

Leonora Thaxton was less ambitious. No doubt she would be content to exchange her body for a pilot's job with his airline. And the way he was aching for her right now, maybe it would be worth giving her a job, Alessandro thought grimly. He knew, of course, that he would do no such thing. His pride would never allow it, and more importantly neither would his duty towards his passengers and customers. He had been too long without a lover—that was all. It was impossible for him to allow himself to want a woman he *knew* was simply using him.

It was a long time before Leonora finally fell asleep, and an even longer time before Alessandro did the same, promising himself that he was going to play Leonora at her own game. Before the weekend was over he intended to prove to her that he could make her want him far more than she could make him want her. No matter how hard she tried to manipulate him she wasn't going to win—and she wasn't going to get a job with his airline either.

CHAPTER TEN

THE bed on which they both lay naked was high, draped with richly sensuous silk fabric. But its touch against her flesh was nowhere near as sensuously erotic as *his* touch, nor could the whisper of the fabric's kiss compare with the fierce passion of *his* kiss.

His face was in the shadows, but she knew its features by heart—from the burning intensity of his dark eyes through the arrogance of his profile to the explicit sensuality of his mouth. Excited pleasure curled and then kicked through her. Simply looking at him awoke and aroused the woman in her in a way and at a level that no other man ever could. Just as she was the only woman who was woman enough to truly complement him as a man. They were made for one another, a perfect match, and they both knew it. Only here, with him, could she truly be herself and let down her guard to share her longing and her love.

He made her ache for him in a thousand—no, a hundred thousand different ways, and the way his knowing smile lifted the corners of his mouth told her that he *knew* that her whole body shuddered in mute delight at the slow, deliberate stroke of his fingertips along the curve of her breast.

He turned his head and looked at her. Joy ran through her like quicksilver as she reached up to him, knowing how much she loved him.

'Alessandro…'

The sound of her own voice woke Leonora from her dream, shocking her into reality, as her cry hung on the morning air of the bedroom. Alessandro her dream lover? How could that be? It couldn't.

She looked towards the other side of the bed. Thankfully it was empty. A glance at her watch told her that she had slept later than normal. She was surprised that she had slept at all, given the events of the evening. There was no sound from the bathroom or the dressing room. She was obviously alone in the bedroom, and of course she was glad. Of course she was. Why had she dreamed about Alessandro like that? She had never even dreamed her fantasy before while sleeping, never mind substituted a real-life man for her imaginary lover.

It didn't mean anything, she reassured herself as she pushed back the bedclothes and stood up. It was only because of what had happened last night before they had gone to bed. It might be true that the more she learned about Alessandro the more she wanted to learn, but that was just because of his airline. It didn't mean that she was foolish enough to think of him as her soul mate. That was ridiculous.

She showered quickly and slightly apprehensively, not wanting either the return of the spider or the return of Alessandro. How awful it would be if he ever got to know about her silly fantasy. But of course he would not get to know. How could he? She certainly wasn't going to tell him, Leonora thought wryly as she dressed casually in her new jeans and one of the T-shirts.

Having brushed her hair and applied a discreet

touch of make-up, she made her way across the courtyard to the main entrance to the house. She was standing in the hallway, wondering what to do about finding some breakfast, when Falcon walked into the hall from the opposite direction, smiling warmly at her when he saw her. Like her, he was dressed casually in jeans, looking younger and less austere than he had done the previous evening.

'No Sandro?' he asked.

'I overslept, I'm afraid, and he must have got impatient for his breakfast,' Leonora responded.

'Most ungallant of him. But most fortunate for me, as it means that I can have the pleasure of escorting you to the breakfast room. With so much going on it will only be a buffet-style affair this morning—although if you wish for something more…'

'No, a light breakfast will be fine,' Leonora assured him.

Alessandro's brother was charming, and handsome, and she felt more comfortable with him than she did with Alessandro himself, but it was Alessandro who made her heart thump against her ribs—just as it was doing now, at the mere thought of him.

'The *castello* is so big I'm sure I'm going to get lost before the weekend's over,' Leonora told her host.

'If you would like a guided tour then I would be happy to be your guide.'

'Oh, no. I didn't mean—I mean, I wasn't...' Flustered, and feeling that she must have sounded as though she was angling for a personal tour of the *castello*, Leonora was aghast. But instead of looking grimly at her, as she was sure Alessandro would have done, Falcon gave her another warm smile and laughed.

'You would prefer Sandro to be the one to escort you, I can see,' he said. 'No, there is no need to deny it. That is just as it should be.'

Alessandro frowned as he stood at the opposite end of the long salon, unobserved by either his brother or Leonora, watching them both. Falcon was smiling warmly at Leonora—too warmly, Alessandro decided—and she was smiling back. Falcon had placed his hand on her arm and she was looking up at him. Out of nowhere a sledgehammer blow fell across Alessandro's heart, momentarily stopping it and then setting it thudding with a fierce, possessive alpha-male anger. Leonora was his, and she was going to stay his.

He was halfway across the room before logic cut in, warning him of the danger he was courting in giving way to his emotions. But by then it was too late, because both Falcon and Leonora had seen him and were looking at him. It was impossible for him to turn back—either from crossing the room or from what he had just learned about himself and his real feelings for Leonora.

'Ah, there you are, Sandro. I found Leonora in the grand hall, looking hungry and alone.'

'I left her in bed, and hungry, I had thought, only for my return.'

Alessandro's response to his brother, his words and their implied meaning, caused Leonora to take a sharp breath at the deliberate sensuality and his implication that there had been an implicit promise between them that he would return to the bed where he had left her to make love to her.

'I did offer to show her round the *castello*, but

she made it plain to me that she would rather you were her guide,' Falcon told his brother without commenting on Alessandro's own words.

Falcon's comment caused Alessandro to look directly at Leonora for the first time since he had joined them. She looked flushed and uncomfortable, as though embarrassed by their conversation, but Alessandro told himself that she was simply putting on an act, that secretly she was relishing the opportunity to make him jealous because Falcon had shown an interest in her. Even so, he had no intention of leaving her on her own with Falcon—or anyone else.

He had risen this morning tired and frustrated, after a largely sleepless night, having at one stage woken up to discover that he had moved to lie so close to Leonora that she'd been within arm's reach of him. His thigh had ached to be thrown over hers, to claim his male possession of her. Of course he had let it do no such thing, moving back to his own side of the bed instead, but the ache had still tormented him—and it was tormenting him now, Alessandro admitted angrily. Of course the only reason he wanted her so fiercely—the only viable reason why his emotions were involved—was because she had challenged him and then rejected him. There was no other permissible reason.

'I thought you might like to see something of the island whilst we're here,' he told Leonora. 'So I've arranged for us to pick up a helicopter at the airfield in half an hour's time. We won't be able to see everything, of course, but I'll do my best to show you the highlights.'

Leonora's face lit up immediately. Unable to conceal her pleasure, she smiled up at Alessandro, her eyes sparkling with excitement.

'I've never piloted a helicopter—' she began, but Alessandro shook his head.

'And you won't be piloting one today either,' he warned her. 'You aren't licensed to fly them.'

'Are you?' Leonora couldn't resist demanding.

'Of course,' Alessandro responded. 'So, either you can have your breakfast now, or we could have brunch at a hotel I know with the most spectacular views of the Ionian Sea.'

'Let the poor girl at least have a cup of

coffee, Sandro,' Falcon protested, but Leonora shook her head.

'Brunch sounds perfect,' she assured Alessandro happily.

In the end she did get her coffee, and some delicious fresh bread and honey, brought to her by Alessandro himself after she had returned to their suite to collect everything she thought she might need.

When he walked in, carrying a tray on which there was a cafetière of coffee, two cups and fresh bread and preserves, she did feel a small sweetly sharp heartbeat of self-conscious uncertainty, brought on as much by her own private dream fantasy as by what had actually happened between them.

The sight of Alessandro dressed like her in jeans, but wearing a soft white short-sleeved linen shirt with them, which somehow emphasised the breadth and masculinity of his torso, heightened her already acute awareness of him. What would happen if she went to him now and told him with the openness and the sexual confidence she knew she ought to have that she could not stop thinking about him and that she wanted them to make love? He had been angry with her last night when she had retreated from him, but he had wanted her then. Did he still want her now?

What was the matter with her? Her virginity might be a burden to her, but that was not a valid reason for her to feel the way she was doing right now. Wanting Alessandro merely physically would have been bad enough, given her ambition to work for him, but the need and the hunger she was battling contained an emotional longing to connect with him.

That was simply because they shared certain aspects of their childhood. She would have felt the same way about any man she met who, like her, was a second child and had lost a parent.

'Here you are.'

She had been so engrossed with her own thoughts that she hadn't noticed that Alessandro had poured them both a cup of coffee. As she took hers from him their fingertips touched, and she had to fight not to reach out to him, to make that touch even more intimate. This was crazy— and dangerous. Anyone would think she'd never been so close to a man before.

She hadn't, though, had she? Or at least not to a sensually powerful and compelling alpha male like Alessandro. He was unique, but her response to him was far from unique, she reminded herself firmly, turning away from him to face the window. She clasped her coffee and pretended to be interested in the view beyond the window in order to avoid having to look at him and further increase her unwanted vulnerability. No doubt hordes of other women had felt about him as she did. But they, unlike her, had no doubt had the sexual confidence to show him how they felt. What would his reaction be if he knew the truth? Would he be as repulsed as she dreaded? Or would he simply laugh at her? Either way, she wasn't going to risk finding out. Not when she already knew that what he certainly *wasn't* likely to do was sweep her up into his arms and carry her to bed. He wouldn't do that, would he? Not after the way she had stopped him last night.

Leonora tightened her grip on her coffee cup,

all too aware of the betraying tremors of longing threatening her body. From the place deep within her memory where she had locked it away came a teasing comment made to her by Leo, when she had first insisted that she wasn't going to give up her dream of working for Alessandro's Avanti Airlines.

'Are you sure it's the job you want and not the man, sis? After all, there are dozens of airlines who'd jump at the chance to take on someone as qualified as you, but the only one *you* seem to be interested in is Alessandro Leopardi's.'

Her response had been immediate. She had repudiated his brotherly teasing, insisting with flags of anger flying in her cheeks that the only reason she was so determined to get Alessandro Leopardi to back down and take her on was to prove a point, that it had nothing to do with the man himself. Or at least not in the way Leo had been implying.

The reality was that her determination to force Alessandro to concede that she was more than up to being one of his pilots had everything to do with the fact that she had been so deeply resentful of his professional rejection of her, and intensely determined to make him change his mind.

'You'd better have something to eat—unless you're one of those women who doesn't do breakfast?'

Alessandro's cool voice, tinged with a mix of disapproval and contempt, broke into the chaotic confusion of her private thoughts. Glad of an excuse not to have to pursue them to a conclusion she already knew she wasn't going to like, Leonora answered him by going over to the table and putting down her coffee before selecting some bread and spreading it with honey.

'Food is fuel for the human body. I wouldn't expect or want to fly an aircraft that wasn't properly fuelled, and the same applies to my body. Besides,' she added wryly, 'it just isn't possible to grow up as the only female in a houseful of men and not eat breakfast. My father used to insist on us all having a huge bowlful of home-made porridge on winter mornings, and to tell the truth it's still my favourite comfort food.' She stopped speaking abruptly, conscious of having allowed him to see a softer side she'd normally have kept hidden.

'Mine is spaghetti with tomato sauce. Falcon used to make it for us—we were often sent supperless to bed by our stepmother, but our old cook taught Falcon how to make a few simple dishes,' Alessandro told her.

They looked at one another, both of them wondering what had prompted them to give away an aspect of themselves they normally kept very carefully guarded. For Alessandro, the unplanned giving of such a confidence about his childhood left him with a need to explain to himself why he had done so. He picked up a piece of bread, spooning fresh preserve onto it and biting into it with strong white teeth in a way that had Leonora's stomach muscles clamping down hard against a surge of sensual heat that caught her off guard.

All he was doing by exchanging such confidences with her was working towards getting her off guard and keeping her there until he was ready to show her which of them was the stronger, Alessandro assured himself, finishing the bread and then telling Leonora crisply, 'I'm surprised you haven't tried for your own helicopter pilot's licence.'

Had he deliberately chosen the word 'tried' to annoy her? Leonora wondered. If so, he had succeeded.

Defensive colour flushed her face as she told him fiercely, 'I had planned to, but tuition is expensive. I don't have the luxury of your kind of wealth. I have to work to support myself—plus, as I don't have a job as a pilot, I have to find the money to keep my licence up to date. Not a lot left over to indulge myself with helicopter piloting tuition.'

'And that's my fault, is it? Because I wouldn't give you a job?' Alessandro mocked her, quickly picking up on what she hadn't said. 'There are other airlines,' he pointed out.

'Not for me. For me there is only you—I mean only Avanti.'

Now Leonora's face was scarlet. What on earth had prompted her to make such a *faux pas* and substitute that far too personal and intimate 'you' for the name of his airline? Her face burning, she looked at Alessandro, but he was looking away from her, casually picking up his coffee as though he hadn't registered what she had said.

Oh, very clever, Alessandro thought cynically, as he pretended not to have registered Leonora's deliberately accidental 'you'. He might not have allowed her to see that he had registered it, but he certainly wasn't fooled by it. She was obviously a member of the 'the best way to a man's heart is via his ego' club, but Alessandro had learned not to trust his own ego a long time ago—and the hard way.

'Mandarin lessons don't come cheap,' he retaliated smoothly. 'And you are, I presume, self-employed?'

Leonora could feel her face burning again, but this time the heat was caused by anger. The parents who paid her to teach their children and the businessmen and -women eager to add Mandarin to their CVs *did* pay well, but she worked hard to fit in as many pupils as she could without prejudicing her own ability to teach them well.

Something her father had taught them all was the need to 'pay back' to society—from being

young they had all run errands for elderly neigh-
bours, as well as worked at home for pocket
money—and now she took that early lesson a
step further and gave as many free lessons as she
could fit in to her timetable, travelling to various
schools to teach groups of financially disadvan-
taged children several nights a week. Not that she
would dream of defending herself from
Alessandro's cutting jibe by telling him that. It
wasn't something she had felt any need to put on
her CV, so why should she feel the need to seek
his good opinion by telling him now?

Unless, of course, there was another reason
she wanted him to approve of her, and like her?
Such as what? She had dreamed about him,
hadn't she? Imagining him as her soul mate. But
that had simply been because of last night, and
didn't mean anything. Heavens, she'd be trying
to tell herself she was in danger of falling in love
with him if she carried on like this.

Her heart did a cartwheel reminiscent of the
first slow spin of a washing machine. Falling in
love with Alessandro? Oh, that would be something, wouldn't it? The joke of the year. And

she'd be the fool—the one everyone was laughing at. But what if it wasn't a joke? What if she was actually falling in love with him? What if she had already fallen in love with him?

Panic gripped her. Her heart went into full washing machine spin cycle. She put down the bread and honey she had been enjoying only a minute ago, unable to finish eating it. Of *course* she hadn't fallen in love with Alessandro. She was panicking over nothing. Just because she had wanted to go to bed with him it didn't mean she loved him. But she had wanted him to hold her. She had wanted—

'We'd better make a move if you're going to see anything much of the island before we have to get back for tonight's ball.'

It was a relief to have Alessandro's voice cutting through the painful confusion of her thoughts.

'Look, I've been thinking.' Leonora gave him her brightest smile. 'If you've got things to do, and I'm going to hold you up, I'm perfectly happy to stay here.'

She wasn't in love with him, but it might be wiser and safer not to spend the day on her own with him.

She wanted to stay here—without him? Alessandro's mouth hardened. Did she really think he was so easily taken in that he didn't know what she was up to? Did she really believe she had a chance with Falcon, or was she simply trying to make him jealous?

'In the hope that Falcon will make good his offer to show you the *castello*?' he asked cynically.

'No,' Leonora denied truthfully.

'Like I said, it's time we made a move,' Alessandro told her, ignoring her denial. Did she really think that he was going to leave her here alone?

They were in the car—a dark green Maserati, all discreet paintwork outside and expensive-smelling leather inside—with Alessandro at the wheel, heading back to the private airstrip along a road Alessandro had told her was a shortcut.

Changing gear to take a series of stomach-churning hairpin bends, his focus was on the road ahead of him as he warned her, 'You are here for one reason and one reason only, and that reason is *not* so that you can flirt with my brother. Remember what I told you about your brother's future if you disobeyed my orders? That still holds good.'

Leonora refused to say anything, looking out of the window and gulping when she saw how steeply the narrow single-track road was dropping as they left the *castello* behind them.

Alessandro held all the power. For Leo's sake she could not defy him. What would she do if he should demand that she give herself to him? He was perfectly capable of making such a demand, she was sure, and of justifying why he had done so. But if he did… The swiftness of her intense physical reaction shocked her. She couldn't possibly *want* him to make such a demand. It would be archaic, appalling, feudal and beyond unthinkable. But if he did, and if she had no option but to let him lead her to his bed and once there command that she give herself over to his will, his touch, his full possession, then what would she do?

What was she thinking about? Or rather *who* was she thinking about? Alessandro wondered grimly as he caught Leonora's small gasp—

surely one of anticipation and pleasure, caused by the privacy of her own thoughts, if the look softening her face was anything to go by. Such a look could not be faked. She probably thought that he was concentrating on his driving too much to be aware of it, but there was nothing about her of which he was not aware—not a look, not a sound, not a scent or a breath, not anything. Everything about her was imprinted into his own senses to irritate and torment him.

Torment? Because she annoyed him so much. Nothing more. His torment was *not* the torment of a man so hungry for a woman that she invaded not just his every thought and feeling but the primary code of his entire being. If he felt anything it was anger—because he knew instinctively that she was thinking about a man she wanted, a man who had already given her sexual pleasure and with whom she was aching to re-experience that pleasure. He was angry that she should think him stupid enough to be taken in by her, and he felt contempt for her as a woman because she clearly could not remain faithful to a man with whom she obviously already had a relationship.

Who was he? *What* was he? The aviation equivalent of a surf bum? One of life's players rather than one of its workers?

Alessandro cut back the speed of the powerful car. He liked well-made pieces of machinery, but he never took risks with them. In his book only a fool did that. The Maserati was one of a kind, adapted from its specifications specifically for him, with a top speed worthy of a race track, but unlike his now-dead half-brother Alessandro had no love of speed for the sake of showing off. And right now the emotions he refused to let himself admit, never mind express, might be urging him to give the car its head and those emotions an outlet, but even with a couple of miles of straight road ahead of him he refused to give in. Alessandro measured himself by a hard code, and he wasn't going to allow any woman to get under his skin enough for him to break it.

They'd reached the airfield, driving past an open hangar in which Leonora could see Alessandro's private jet. The helicopter was standing out on the tarmac, its Avanti Airlines paintwork of silver on white gleaming in the brilliance of the morning sunshine.

Alessandro brought the car to a halt outside the impressive architecture of a modern and chrome building that somehow, despite its stylish and almost urban modern look, seemed to fit perfectly into the landscape.

Alessandro noticed Leonora studying the building. Falcon, who had trained as an architect, and who shared his own love of structure and design, had incorporated many of Alessandro's own ideas into his design for the small terminal and office building, which also had its own air traffic control unit. Alessandro did a substantial amount of business with various concerns on the island, and for a variety of reasons had decided to construct his own private airfield rather than be dependent on the island's public airport facilities.

In addition to keeping the helicopter permanently based on the island, Alessandro also funded an air ambulance service, and provided the air ambulance itself. He and his brothers were united in their determination to do what they could to offset the effect of their father's feudal grip on his land and on the people who depended on it and him for their livelihood.

Falcon worked tirelessly behind the scenes to try and improve the lot of young people who otherwise would have no future ahead of them other than that endured by their parents and their grandparents. And in addition to the building work he was already doing on the island Rocco—helped by funds from Falcon and Alessandro—was building what would eventually be a college that they all hoped would be a gateway for at least some of the island's young people to a different way of life. Alessandro already had on his payroll several young men from his father's villages, whom he had trained at his own expense as aircraft technicians. All the staff working at the airfield came from local families and were paid well.

'I just want to check over everything with the ops crew,' he informed Leonora, before he opened the door of the car.

A smiling member of the ground staff opened Leonora's door for her. Not sure whether she was supposed to stand around and wait or follow him, Leonora opted for the latter course, hurrying to catch up with Alessandro as he strode across the concrete apron.

Inside the building air-conditioning cooled the air to exactly the right temperature and a smartly dressed and very pretty receptionist welcomed Alessandro. Leonora's attention was focused on the Leonardo da Vinci prints decorating the off-white walls opposite the tinted glass frontage of the building.

Seeing her looking at the prints, Alessandro told her, 'They are copies of Leonardo's sketches for various forms of flight.'

'Yes, I know,' Leonora responded, nodding in the direction of the prints as she told him, 'Whilst other girls were putting pin-ups of pop stars on their bedroom walls, mine were decorated with those. I found a set in a second-hand shop and badgered the poor shop owner until he eventually agreed to let me have them in exchange for working there on Saturdays.'

Alessandro looked away from her.

'I bought my first set during a visit to Florence to see my mother's relatives. My stepmother ripped them down from my bedroom wall and burned them as punishment for my not bringing back a gift for Antonio.'

'Oh, how cruel.' Her indignation made Leonora's voice shake, and instinctively she reached out and put her hand on Alessandro's arm—only to remove it as quickly as though she had been burned.

Stiffening, he drew back from her, and walked towards the pretty receptionist without a backwards look. Did she really think that he was taken in by her false sympathy?

Alessandro shrugged aside the warning slamming his heartbeat into his chest and telling him that his reactions to Leonora were both illogical and dangerous.

CHAPTER ELEVEN

THEY'D been in the air for nearly two hours. She'd seen Mount Etna from above, holding her breath as Alessandro took them in close to the volcano, and the remains of architectural wonders built by the many civilisations that had come to this island and left their stamp on it. Alessandro had given her a potted history of the island's differing cultures, and she'd heard the cynicism in his voice when he'd touched briefly on the feudal aspects of his own family's role in Sicily's history.

They'd flown over Palermo, spread beneath them in all its faded glory, with its groves of citrus fruit and olives, and now they were heading for the coast and the hotel where they were going to have what would now be lunch rather than brunch.

'Falcon was chief architect for the hotel to which we are heading, and Rocco, my younger brother, was the builder. It is part of a new fraternal venture—of sorts—a luxury resort on Capo d'Orlando, close to the town of Cefalù and overlooking the Tyrrhenian Sea. My contribution was the helipad and direct helicopter access from the island's airport to the resort. We are also looking into providing helicopter access to the Aeolian Islands offshore. If you look to your right now you should see the headland.'

Obediently Leonora did as Alessandro suggested, exclaiming, 'Oh, how beautiful!' when she saw the small cape, its sandy beaches lapped by turquoise waves. Cefalù resort itself was a picturesque tumble of clusters of Mediterranean colour-washed buildings, basking in the sunshine.

'This part of the island has known many civilisations, but for this development it was decided that we would follow a Moorish style of architecture. Here is the helipad, coming up now,' Alessandro added, in between speaking to the control unit, giving his position and getting clearance for landing.

He circled a tall tower that rose high above the rest of the sand-coloured complex below them, skilfully hovering over the landing pad before dropping the helicopter perfectly onto it. The tower and its landing pad combined both the beauty of ancient architecture and the near miracle of modern aero science, Leonora recognised, as she listened to Alessandro finishing his touchdown procedures with the control unit.

Outside, the ground staff were waiting to go through their checks, and as soon as Alessandro had stopped speaking he opened his door and got out of the helicopter. Leonora went to open her own door, but before she could get out Alessandro was there, offering her a helping hand. Initially tempted to refuse it, she reminded herself instead of the role she was supposed to be playing. And of course that was the *only* reason why she was allowing Alessandro to hold her. Her decision certainly had nothing whatsoever to do with that cartwheel of her heart, followed by the dizzy burst of pleasure engendered by his touch. Not at all.

So why was she almost leaning into him, and so delaying the moment when he could release her?

She wanted so badly to stay where she was, leaning into him, free to breathe in the scent of him, free to place her hand just above his heart and feel its strong, fierce beat. When a woman truly loved a man this was all she wanted: his closeness, their oneness, the knowledge that no other man could take his place. But she did not *love* Alessandro—truly or otherwise.

How could this woman get beneath his guard so easily and so disruptively? Alessandro wondered grimly. How could he possibly be thinking that he was sorry their flight was over because he had enjoyed the intimacy and the conversation they had shared so very much?

'This way.'

Alessandro might not be holding her close any more, but he was still holding her hand.

'There's a lift down to the hotel foyer over here,' Alessandro informed Leonora, guiding her towards an elegant limestone staircase that descended from the floor of the helipad into a smart forecourt.

Within seconds of stepping into the lift they were stepping out of it again, into the hotel foyer, beyond which Leonora could see a very smart restaurant and cocktail bar, and beyond that a wide terrace overlooking the sea.

Several tables were already occupied, but the one to which they were shown had by far the best position, Leonora noted. A tall, impeccably groomed woman, whose appearance—in Leonora's opinion, at least—was slightly marred by the amount of clanking gold jewellery she was wearing, turned her head to look at them.

'Alessandro!' she exclaimed. 'But how wonderful. I was only just talking about you to Luca, saying how much I was looking forward to seeing you again.'

Ignoring Leonora, the woman embraced Alessandro, lingering over the exchange of supposedly merely polite friendly kisses, and then retaining her hold of Alessandro's arm.

'It was such a wonderful surprise when your father invited me to attend the ball. I am looking forward to it so much. You will remember Luca, my cousin, of course?'

Alessandro inclined his head politely but distantly. Sofia was the last person he had been expecting to see when he had walked into the restaurant. How typical of his father that he should have invited *her* to attend tonight's celebratory ball. No doubt he had hoped to add a fresh sting of pain to old wounds, but he was wasting his time. How typical of him to do such a thing—and how pointless. Looking at her, and listening to her now, Alessandro could only marvel that he had ever found her in any way attractive. He could see the avarice in her gaze, could feel it in the possessive clutch of her hand on his arm.

Her cousin, he seemed to remember, had a long history of being her escort when she had no husband in tow, and the gossip was that they slept together as well, when neither had anyone else to share a bed with. Luca, a decade older than Sofia, which took him close to fifty, with a perma-tan and flesh like a snake's, was focusing his attention on Leonora. Instantly Alessandro stepped towards her, ignoring his ex-lover's possessive drag on his arm to say curtly, 'Please excuse us, Sofia, but we have had a busy morning, and I know that Leonora is ready for her lunch.'

'Leonora?' Sofia questioned—for all the world

as though she hadn't even noticed that she was there, Leonora thought grimly, as the other woman smiled up at Alessandro.

'My…partner,' Alessandro informed Sofia firmly.

His *partner*? In what? In lies and deceit, yes. But in the real sense of the word, as Alessandro was quite obviously implying, then she was no such thing.

But Leonora was speedily adding two and two together, from the broad hints Sofia had given as to the nature of her old relationship with Alessandro and the comment Alessandro himself had made to her about a past love who had let him down. And she was coming to the natural conclusion that at one time Alessandro and Sofia had been lovers. Alessandro now—no doubt out of male pride—wanted Sofia to think that Leonora was enjoying her old position in his life—and in his bed. Had Alessandro known that Sofia was likely to be attending the ball? Was that the main reason he had blackmailed Leonora into partnering him?

What if it was? What did it matter to her what

his reason was? But it *did* matter, Leonora admitted miserably, unable to stop comparing herself to the elegant and self-confident Sofia, who was now holding on to Alessandro's arm for all the world as though they were still a couple, forcing Leonora to one side. Leonora found herself wanting. Sofia had an air about her that said quite plainly that she was a very sexually experienced and knowing woman. The kind of woman Alessandro would much rather have in his bed than an inexperienced woman like her.

'I'm sure Leonora won't mind if we join you for lunch. This is a wonderful hotel. Your father was kind enough to recommend it. He told me that you and your brothers own it, Alessandro.'

Alessandro part owned the hotel too? Well, that was more than he had told her, Leonora reflected. But perhaps she should have worked that out for herself, after what he had told her about their fraternal input into it. Just as she should also have worked out that there was more to his insistence that she partner him to the weekend's events than he had told her.

How his father would have loved seeing the

result of his meddling, Alessandro thought grimly as he was forced to allow Sofia to thrust her unwanted company on them. He knew that he had been emotionally and physically naive when he had first met her, but now meeting her again after so many years, he acknowledged wryly that he must have been even more naive than he had thought for ever having found her remotely attractive. Seen side by side with Leonora she looked tawdry and cheap, as fake as the 'designer label' handbags sold in the street markets of Florence to gullible tourists. Her gossip as they waited for the table to be enlarged was littered with references to people and places favoured by the celebrity culture he so despised and loathed, and by the time they were finally seated Alessandro was longing for the pure, clear bite of Leonora's far more varied and interesting conversation.

'So, Leonora, how long have you known Sandro? He and I were close for a long time, and I don't think it's any secret that he would have asked me to marry him if I'd let him. We were so young then, though—too young to know how lucky we were to have met one another. And of course as I was still modelling then I travelled a great deal, and poor Alessandro became very jealous of all the handsome rich men who wanted to take me out—didn't you, darling?'

'I'm afraid I don't remember,' Alessandro told her. 'After all, as you said yourself, it was a long time ago.'

'Oh, come on, Sandro,' Luca put in. 'You were mad for Sofia and we all knew it. I remember that diamond bracelet you bought her from Cartier. You desperately wanted to buy her a ring as well, but I told you you should talk to her first.'

Leonora, who *had* been feeling hungry, discovered that she had lost her appetite. It was ridiculous to feel so painfully jealous of a relationship that was in the past and a man she could never have, and yet she did. And it hurt—dreadfully.

'They serve locally caught fish here. I can recommend it,' Alessandro advised Leonora, ignoring Luca's comment. He had forgotten all about the Cartier bangle—bought not on a whim, he remembered now, but because Sofia had hinted so very broadly that she wanted it. There had certainly never been any discussion about a ring. Not that he could claim that he would *not* have bought her one during those early months of their relationship, before he had realised the truth about her.

'What is your costume for tonight, Sandro? I'm so excited about the ball. It's such a hugely prestigious event, and so exclusive.'

'Hardly, Sofia. It is a private celebration of a historical family event, that's all. Not one of your celebrity affairs.'

Sofia pouted.

'*Caro*, you are being far too modest. I understood from your father that at least two top-magazine society-page editors had been invited.'

That was news to Alessandro—unwelcome news. He suspected that it would be equally unwelcome to Falcon. Yet another example of their father's love of meddling. He'd have to warn Falcon to check the guest list.

'Who are you impersonating?' Alessandro asked Sofia, adding, 'No—let me guess—Lucretia Borgia?'

She gave a sharp trill of laughter.

'That is so naughty of you, Sandro—you always did have a wicked sense of humour. No, actually, I shall be Napoleon's sister Pauline—the bride your ancestor wanted for his son. Has Alessandro told you anything of the history of his family yet, Leonora?'

'A little—' Leonora began.

But Alessandro spoke over her answer, saying coolly, 'We've been far too busy talking about our own future to delve into the ancient past.'

'Ah, *caro*, do you remember the plans we had for our future?' Sofia asked Alessandro softly, placing her hand on his arm.

They deserved one another, Leonora decided crossly an hour later, as she sat pushing her lunch round her plate and trying not to feel sorry for herself. She listened to Alessandro and Sofia. For all that Alessandro's responses to her were blunt and dismissive, plainly Sofia believed that he still cared about her—otherwise surely she would not be so persistent. Leonora certainly believed that he did—even if for his pride's sake he was trying to pretend that he did not.

They were the last to leave the restaurant, Sofia

having insisted on extending their lunch well into the afternoon, although having failed to persuade Alessandro into agreeing that she could move from the hotel to the *castello*. She had also failed to persuade him to go up to her suite with her so that she could show him how much she still treasured the Cartier bangle, which she apparently had with her.

Alessandro and Leonora flew back to the *castello* almost in silence, and when Alessandro told her that he had something he needed to discuss with his brother Leonora was glad of the opportunity to escape to their suite on her own, so that she could deal in private with the discovery she had made before they had left the hotel.

They had been in the foyer, saying their goodbyes after lunch. Sofia naturally had been all over Alessandro, but it had been when Leonora had seen the other woman kissing Alessandro on the mouth with a deliberate sensuality that had had his hands lifting to grip her arms that the hideous truth had torn through her. She loved him. How, when and why were all questions she could not answer. But they didn't affect the reality and its unbearable truth. Somehow, without her wanting it to happen and without her knowing how it had happened, he had taken her heart as effortlessly as his ancestors had taken their people's lands.

Leonora had always believed that she possessed both common sense and determination, but neither of them were strong enough to prevent the flow of some very painful tears in the privacy of the suite, as she lay curled up on the bed she had shared with Alessandro as his black-mailed pretend mistress. She would never share it with him as a woman who loved him, and who was loved by him in return.

She should take the opportunity to shower and wash her hair and ready herself for the evening before Alessandro returned. What would happen tonight? Would they still share this room or, despite all that he had said to Sofia over lunch, would Sofia be the one sharing his bed tonight?

CHAPTER TWELVE

As ALESSANDRO headed for the West Tower Suite his mind was on the conversation he had just had with Falcon. He had gone to find his brother, to warn him about what their father had done, and Falcon had been every bit as angry about their father's surreptitious invitation to Sofia as Alessandro had known he would be.

'I don't want her here tonight,' Alessandro had told Falcon. 'In fact I'd even go and tell Father that if I'd known she would be here then I would have refused to attend the ball if it weren't for the fact that he'd be bound to assume that I couldn't bear to be in the same room as a woman I once loved and lost. The only feelings I have left for Sofia are those of disbelief that I was ever taken in by her, and a certain dislike of admitting that I didn't recognise what she was in the first place so you had to rescue me from her.'

'I know that has always rankled, Sandro,' Falcon had surprised him by saying. And then he had gone on to surprise him even further by adding, 'I have often regretted my interference, and my inability to control the desire to play the big brother who knew what was best for you. You have always had the most carefully honed instincts of all of us, and it is my belief that in your heart you were already aware of what Sofia really was. But of course in those days my ego did tend to push me into interfering where my interference wasn't needed. No doubt an attempt to assert my position and to comfort myself that, even though you were an adult, you still needed me. For so long you and Rocco were my *raison d'être* so to speak—the purpose of my determination not to give in to our father. I became very good at telling myself I was doing things for your sakes and not my own, and with your adulthood came the fear of what my purpose in life would be other than my tethered goat status as eldest son and heir. With every step you took towards independence from our father I felt my own status crumble a little more.'

Falcon had reached out and put his hand on Alessandro's arm in a loving fraternal clasp. 'I have never said so before, and I have blamed myself many times for not doing so, but I needed you, Sandro—I needed your strength and your support and I was very afraid of losing them. Foolish of me, since those things we shared as boys still bond us together today, even though we seldom speak of them, and I still think of you as my strong right arm, and in fact as my true strength.'

Alessandro stopped in mid-step, as overcome by emotion now as he had been when he had heard Falcon say those words—miraculous, beneficent, humbling words that had filled him with love and given him a truly precious gift.

In answer to Falcon's emotional speech he had reached out in turn, placing his free hand on Falcon's arm and clasping it, as Falcon had, so that they were locked together. Then they had released one another and come together in a fierce, loving hug.

'I have looked up to you all my life, Falcon— and, yes, envied you as well. Not because you are the first-born, and certainly not because of what you will inherit, but because of your great courage and everything that you are. You are my hero, the person I have always longed most to be.'

'I doubt that your Leonora would be very happy to see the man she obviously loves so much changed in any kind of way. I envy you that, Sandro—a woman who loves you for what you are and not what you have, but also a woman with whom you have so much in common and can share your life. Be happy, my brother, for happiness is the greatest gift life can give us, and it is the one you deserve more than most. We must none of us repeat our father's mistakes. His bitterness and resentment mark him like a physical brand.'

'He has accepted now that Antonio did not father a child?'

'Reluctantly. As you know, I have looked thoroughly into every relationship Antonio had at the time, that would have allowed a child to have been conceived—in the period when he claims the child *was* conceived—even those lasting no more than a matter of hours. The facts prove beyond any doubt that there is no child.'

They had embraced again, but it hadn't been the breaking down of barriers that had allowed them to reach out to one another and show their love for one another that had occupied Alessandro's thoughts as much as Falcon's comments about Leonora. She didn't love him. Falcon was wrong about that. But they did have a great deal in common, he did desire her and he was certain that she desired him.

What if he suggested to her that they started again as two people who shared a mutual interest and a mutual desire that could, if they chose, go on to the mutual and exclusive intimacy of them becoming lovers who might ultimately commit to one another? Inside his head he had a mental image of the two of them together, of him holding her naked in their shared bed. She was smiling at him, her hair spilling over his body, her expression soft with love and happiness. An extraordinary sense of freedom and joy filled him, softening all the hard, painful edges of doubt and suspicion.

They could be lovers. Lovers who could meet equally in the neutral territory of shared honesty—a territory where they could put aside the contentious issues that kept them apart.

To do that, though, he would have to reveal to her his feelings and his desire, and in doing so risk appearing vulnerable. He would have to be the one who took the first step and showed his need and his weakness. Did he want her enough to take that risk?

As he continued to stride down the corridor, Alessandro knew the answer to his own question.

As for Sofia, he and Falcon had come to a decision to have an immediate message sent to the hotel where Sofia was staying, bluntly telling her that her invitation had been rescinded, and warning her that she would be refused entry if she attempted to attend the ball.

Their costumes were hanging ready in the dressing room—Alessandro's that of a fierce Norman warrior and her own that of a Saracen princess. Was she going to be able to get through the evening ahead of them without humiliating herself because of her love for Alessandro? She had felt so desperately jealous this afternoon, forced to sit and watch and listen whilst Sofia flirted with him, knowing that once they had been lovers and that Alessandro probably still loved her now.

She might not be free to announce that she was leaving, but there was one decision she could and had made—and that was that she no longer intended to pursue her dream to work for Alessandro's airline. How could she, now that she knew how she felt about him? She would never be able to concentrate properly on her work, and if she ever had to fly *him* anywhere she would be so wrought up with longing for him that she simply would not be able to be professional. Her dream was over. The harsh reality of her uninvited and unrequited love had destroyed it.

When Alessandro opened the door into the suite, Leonora was standing by the window, looking out.

'Checking to see if your spider friend is making a return trip?' he asked her.

The gently teasing note in his voice brought the

swift sting of too-emotional tears to Leonora's eyes. Blinking fiercely, she half turned round, shaking her head.

'There's something I want to discuss with you,' Alessandro told her. 'It's about your desire to work for me.' *And my desire for you*, he was tempted to say. But he didn't want to antagonise her by rushing things.

'I've changed my mind about that,' Leonora told him simply. 'I don't want to work for you any more.' *Because I love you too much to bear the pain of seeing you but not being with you.*

Her statement was so unexpected and so obviously heartfelt that it made him pause and look searchingly at her. She looked pale and strained.

'Why not?'

'I'd really rather not say.'

'You've bombarded me with applications and your CV for two years, and now suddenly, just like that, you don't want a job with me after all and you won't say why?' He shook his head. 'If this is some kind of change of tactic, designed to make me—'

'No, it isn't.'

There was a catch in her voice that checked him. Something was very wrong. She wasn't simply trying a new strategy.

'What's wrong?' he asked her. 'You don't look well.'

'Nothing's wrong.'

'Liar,' he said, going to her and putting his hands on her shoulders.

He had intended to turn her in to the light, so that he could look at her more closely, but immediately she pulled away from him with a small gasp, retreating into the shadows and then saying too quickly, 'Our costumes are in the dressing room. You are to be a Norman knight, and I am a Saracen princess according to the labels on them.'

'Yes,' he agreed. 'When my family first came to Sicily as Norman knights my ancestor took as his mistress the daughter of the Saracen lord who held this land before he was vanquished.'

Leonora looked at him, and then looked away again, but it was too late. Alessandro had seen the desire in her gaze.

He moved closer to her, wearing his confidence with ease, backing her into a corner as he told her softly, 'I want us to have a fresh start, Leonora—I want us to be lovers.'

Her heart was a single, tight, unbearable ache inside her chest. To be offered what she so much desired and to know that she must refuse was truly a pain in a class of its own.

'No.'

'You want me,' Alessandro insisted.

'It must have been a shock for you to see Sofia at lunchtime.'

'My father would have liked to think so.'

'She's the woman you told me about, isn't she? The one you loved?'

Alessandro frowned. Why were they discussing Sofia, when all he wanted to do was take her in his arms?

'I may have thought once that I loved her, but I was wrong. And I don't want to waste time talking about Sofia when I could be holding you.'

She couldn't bear this. She really couldn't.

'No,' she protested, but Alessandro shook his head and framed her face in his hands, kissing her slowly and thoroughly. When he felt the sweet, sensual shudder grip her he kissed her more deeply, his tongue finding hers, his body closing in on hers.

Please, just let me have this, Leonora begged fate. Just these few kisses, and the erotically powerful weight of his body backing her own against the wall whilst his hands slipped from her face to hold her body and shield it from any discomfort. Somehow—how?—her thighs knew how to part for his even whilst her arms wrapped round him. His hands stroked from her back to her breasts, caressing them slowly and rhythmically until she was near mindless with a pleasure that could only demand more, wanting the intimacy of his touch on her bare skin.

She had no words for her need, only the frantic pleading of her lips against his jaw and then his throat, her tongue-tip tasting the male saltiness of his skin and tracing the swell of his Adam's apple. She pushed away his shirt, her hands trembling as she explored the shape of his back, smoothing her whole hand, palm flat, over his flesh, wanting to absorb the feel of every single cell of him, to commit that sensation to her memory.

She pressed her lips, open and hungry, to the

bared vee of flesh exposed by his shirt, burying her face against him, shaking with a need that was as intensely emotional as it was physical. She could feel the swollen hard jut of his sex pressing against her softness. The ache of her own need pierced her, making her want to cry. In her mind's eye she could see him and feel him, taking that ache to an unbearable intensity with the slow and then fast thrust of his body within her own flesh, soothing it, satisfying it, filling her with a pleasure so perfect that it lifted them both to another dimension.

He was her soul mate. Not a fantasy lover any more, but a real man—far more perfect in every way than the shadowy figure she had once imagined.

The touch of Leonora's hands and mouth on his skin was pushing Alessandro beyond the limits of his self-control, taking him to a place with a promise of pleasure he'd never known or imagined might exist.

Alessandro tugged up the hem of the T-shirt Leonora had changed into after her shower, pulling it over her head and exposing her braless breasts. Bending his head, he captured one hard, swollen nipple with his lips, caressing it with his tongue-tip as he cupped her other breast in his hand, licking and sucking on her nipple until she was crying out in frantic pleasure. His fingers drew the same delight from her other breast, rendering her mindless and helpless, but when he unfastened the button on her jeans and unzipped them, sliding his hand down over her quivering belly and against her sex, Leonora knew she had to stop him or face the humiliation of him discovering she was a virgin and then rejecting her.

She had to stop him—yes. But please not yet—not now, when he was touching her with such unbelievable erotic intimacy, his fingertip finding the quivering eagerness of her clitoris.

She was velvet and roses, the scent of night and the eternal lure of the tide that moved the sea. She was woman, *his* woman, and he loved her more than he thought possible.

This was too much. She had to stop him now, whilst she was still able. Frantically Leonora pushed at Alessandro's chest, her heart thudding with a mixture of exertion and unbearable grief, heavy with love and longing, and with the dread of what she must do.

She wanted him to stop. She didn't want him. She didn't love him.

Alessandro had thought he knew the meaning of despair and loss, but he realised now he had not known them at all. He could feel his hands trembling as he released her. His throat was raw and his voice harsh as the plea he had promised he would not make burst from his throat in an agonised plea.

'Why? You want me! I know you do. If this is some game…'

Leonora shook her head. She didn't want to tell him, but the intimacy they had just shared could not be put aside—and besides, she was incurably honest.

'It isn't a game. Yes, I do want you. But you wouldn't want me if you knew the truth about me. I'm so ashamed. It's so humiliating. No man would want me if they knew, but especially a man like you.'

Tears thickened her voice.

What had she done? What secrets were there in her past that caused her such shame?

'If there have been others then that is only natural. But—'

Leonora started to laugh almost hysterically. She couldn't help it.

'Of course it is only natural. That's the whole point. There *haven't* been any others. I am not natural. I'm *unnatural*. What else can I be when I'm still a virgin?'

The air in the room seemed to thicken and go still. Alessandro looked at her, his heartbeat thudding, quickening from arousal to disbelief.

'You're a virgin?'

'Yes,' Leonora told him in a brittle voice, tossing her head. The defensive tomboy was stirring back to life. 'Ridiculous, isn't it? Perhaps I should wear a sign saying "Men beware. Virgin at large". It's all right, you don't have to say anything. I know how you feel. After all no man of your experience wants to go to bed with a virgin past her sell-by date. You want a woman you can enjoy having sex with— someone who can pleasure you as much as you can her. Not a…a woman like me who isn't even a proper woman…'

A virgin. She was a virgin. And she was hurting because of it, fearing his mockery and his rejection.

'You're right,' he told her softly. 'I *do* want a woman in my bed I can enjoy having sex with— a woman who can pleasure me as much as I intend to pleasure her, a woman who loves and desires me as much as I do her.'

He reached for her hand and she let him take it, unable to do anything other than let the pain roll down over her, crushing her and yet leaving her alive to experience even more pain.

'You *are* that woman, Leonora—my woman.'

'No,' she protested, not daring to believe him and certain that what he was saying was some kind of cruel joke.

'Yes.'

'But I'm not sensual, or skilled, or experienced like Sofia.'

Alessandro made a dismissive contemptuous sound deep in his throat. 'Sofia is as hard as nails and just about as sensual. True sensuality does not come from sexual experience but from within, from being with a partner who arouses it and shares it. Falcon was saying to me earlier how much he envies me because you and I share so much in common. I am not a virgin, but there is within me because of my childhood a desire— a need, in fact—to know that what is mine belongs only to me. Had you had ten lovers or a hundred it could not and would not have changed my love for you. But knowing that you have not, and that you will be exclusively mine, is a gift I never hoped to have. It is a soothing balm against a running sore within my psyche, the existence of which I have never been able to admit to myself until now, never mind to anyone else. Knowing I will not have to compete with any other man in your past...' Alessandro shook his head. 'I am ashamed to admit these things to you because of what they say about me.'

'No, you mustn't be,' Leonora assured him.

She *did* understand. She knew what he was revealing to her didn't spring from mere male ego or vanity but instead was something that went much deeper—a vulnerability within him, some might say a flaw, that only made him all the more human and loveable to her.

Even as her heart sang with the revelation that

he loved her, she said, 'I don't want to disappoint you.'

'You will never disappoint me.'

He undressed her slowly and tenderly, encouraging her to undress him and then touch him, taking pleasure in her pleasure, taking time to reassure her. And in the end she was the one who urged him to possess her, crying out as she arched up against him, wrapping her long slim legs around him, her body knowing instinctively what it wanted from him and how to elicit it.

He thrust into her carefully, with the pad of his thumb finding her clitoris and caressing it as the pace of his rhythmic thrusts increased. Leonora clung to him, her breathing fast and shallow, her chest flushed with sexual desire, her whole being focused on their shared pleasure.

The convulsions began as he thrust deeper, making her cry out to him, imploring urgently, 'Deeper, Alessandro. Deeper and harder—yes, like that. Just like that.'

The convulsions gripped tighter and the thrust of his flesh within her own carried her over the threshold into full womanhood without her

knowing anything other than the spiralling ex-
ploding miracle of her orgasm and the rhythmic
surge that took him to his own completion.

Breathless, satiated, brimming over with joy
and triumph, Leonora clung to Alessandro's
naked and sweat-slick body, her head resting on
his shoulder whilst her heartbeat raced, her heart
itself filled to overflowing with the strength and
the power of her love for him.

Never had she imagined that she might feel so
blessed, so complete. There was no past nor any
future, no doubt and no fear, only the wonderful
and perfect rightness of the shared here and now.

She reached up and touched Alessandro's face,
her own illuminated with all that she was feeling.

Alessandro was looking down at her, his face
shadowed.

Her 'thank you' lilted, caught with the sweet-
ness of her joy.

'We should get ready for the ball, otherwise
we're going to be late,' Alessandro warned her,
withdrawing from her, knowing that if he didn't
it was unlikely they would put in an appearance
at all. 'I don't want to let Falcon down.'

'No, of course not,' Leonora agreed valiantly.

She wasn't going to allow herself to feel disappointed or to regret anything just because he hadn't said anything about them sharing a future. It would be naive of her to think that his words of love to her earlier had been intended as a commitment. She must just be happy with what she had with him now, the fact that he loved her now, and not think about anything else.

Two hours later, with Alessandro on one side of his father and Falcon on the other, as she stood with Alessandro in the receiving line, greeting the arriving guests, Leonora was torn between pride and pain. Pride because she was Alessandro's, and pain because she knew that their shared time together might only be short.

The last of the guests had been received and welcomed. The quartet who had been playing in the background went to join the rest of the musicians in a specially designed alcove in the ballroom. The ballroom itself shimmered in the light of dozens of candles in elegant silver-gilt candelabra on the walls between the matching silver-gilt-framed mirrors. The scent of the white lilies and the greenery that made up the stunningly beautiful floral decorations filled the air.

The musicians struck up the first notes of a waltz and the guests, who had fallen back towards the walls, to leave the length of the ballroom floor free, turned expectantly to look towards their hosts. To Leonora's surprise, Alessandro turned to her, making her a small, formal half-bow.

He looked magnificent, in a medieval-style tunic of crimson cloth embroidered with the Leopardi arms worn over a grey undershirt, and a short cloak of scarlet lined with gold flowing from his shoulders. On a man of less male and athletic build such a costume would have looked ridiculous, but on Alessandro it looked magnificent. He was the first Leopardi, the powerful virile conqueror who had captured her heart and demanded his right to her body.

Leonora felt the breath lock in her lungs as he reached for her hand. Her own costume of several layers of the sheerest silk in varying shades of gold and bronze seemed to move with the thud of her heart. Eyes downcast, she allowed Alessandro to lead her onto the floor, hesitating only when he fully claimed her, taking her into his arms. Her gaze flew to his and she felt her body trembling as though she really was the Saracen princess whose virginity he had taken—as though in giving him her hand in public view she was like that princess, allowing him to show his people that he had claimed her for himself.

They danced alone, and Leonora was more conscious of the intimacy of his hold and her own fierce longing for it than she was of the whispered comments of their audience. Her gaze never left his face, her every breath saying how completely and proudly she had given herself to him and how totally she trusted him.

Alessandro drew her closer. She was *his*. He had claimed her in the privacy of his bed, and now he was claiming her in public.

After they had finished dancing, and the guests had clapped their performance enthusiastically, the musicians struck up again and the floor filled with dancers, allowing Alessandro to talk briefly and politely with some of the guests, whilst always keeping Leonora at his side.

For Leonora the evening passed in a daze of golden joy, highlighted by precious private moments carefully stored in her memory.

She must have talked, eaten, drunk at least some of the champagne she had been served, although she had no real recollection of doing so. All she knew and all she wanted to know was Alessandro.

'It will soon be midnight,' he told her, 'and Falcon is planning to make an important announcement. It's been too long since I kissed you. Will you be cold if we go out on the terrace?'

Leonora shook her head. What did it matter how cold she might be if Alessandro wanted to kiss her?

The doors to the terrace were locked, but Alessandro had the key, and Leonora noticed that he locked the doors behind them, so that they wouldn't be interrupted. The sky was so clear that she felt she could almost have reached out and touched the stars.

'You look lovely. You *are* lovely, Leonora—in every single way. I felt so proud tonight, having you at my side.'

'No. I was the one who felt proud to be with you,' Leonora told him.

She could see him smiling as he drew her close and kissed her, slowly and tenderly.

'I wish we could go back to our room,' Leonora whispered.

'You're a temptress—you know that, don't you?' Alessandro's voice was thick with passion. He squeezed her hand and told her, almost unsteadily, 'You remember I told you that my ancestor took the daughter of the Saracen he had vanquished as his mistress?'

Leonora nodded her head.

'What I didn't get round to telling you,' he informed her, shifting her weight in his arms so that he could look down into her face, 'was that he also made her his wife. You see, he fell in love with her—just as I have done with you. Marry me, Leonora.'

'You want to *marry* me?'

'Yes. And you've got exactly five minutes to

make up your mind, because if the answer is no then I shall have to find Falcon and stop him announcing our engagement. I told him earlier that I love you, and that I want you to be my wife, and I can't think of any better way to tell the world than to make an announcement here tonight of our commitment to one another. If you are willing?'

She pretended to look grave.

'There's a condition,' she warned him.

Alessandro didn't care. She could make any condition she liked—including insisting on being the one to fly them when they travelled. All that mattered to him now was that she was his. She completed him, made him whole, and he had been a fool not to realise that the very first time he had read her job application and looked at her photograph.

'Mmm,' he murmured, as he lifted her hand to his lips and kissed her palm and then each finger in turn. 'What condition?'

'You must promise never, *ever* to tell my brothers about that spider.'

'What spider?'

'And I want us to have an even number of children so that there is no middle child.'

'Two, you mean?'

'Or four, or maybe even six.'

It was two minutes to midnight. Just enough time for Alessandro to kiss her with fierce exultation and commitment, and then reach into his pocket for a worn leather jeweller's box.

'If you don't like this then you shall have something else of your own choice,' Alessandro told her, opening the box. 'But this ring belonged to my great-great-grandmother on my mother's side. It is said that she married the man she loved and that their marriage was long and happy.'

The flawless single diamond on a plain gold band caught the light and captured it, holding it deep in its heart.

'It's beautiful and I love it,' Leonora told him truthfully.

When Alessandro slid it onto her finger the gold felt warm, almost caressing her finger, making her feel it was a true symbol of their love.

There was just time for one more all too brief kiss, and then Alessandro was guiding her back into the ballroom. Waiters were already circulating with trays holding glasses of champagne, and Falcon was waiting to lead them into the centre of the room.

'Ladies and gentlemen,' he began. 'Honoured friends and guests. It is my delight and my privilege to announce the engagement of my brother Alessandro Leopardi to Miss Leonora Thaxton. Please raise your glasses with me to Alessandro and to his wife-to-be, Leonora.'

When Alessandro held out his own glass to her, in a symbolic gesture of intimacy and promise, so that she could drink from it, Leonora trembled from head to foot with happiness.

'Your father is watching us,' Leonora whispered.

Alessandro turned his head to look at him.

'He looks so old and alone,' Leonora told him.

'Yes, but it is a situation of his own making. I don't want to talk about the past. I want to live in the present and in the future—with you, Leonora. I love you so much.'

'And I you.'

Leonora's breath quickened. Suddenly all she wanted was for them to be able to slip away to the privacy of their suite, where they could make their vows of love to one another in private.

Falcon watched them. It was obvious that they were madly in love with one another. Alessandro had eyes only for Leonora and she for him. Both his brothers had found love and wanted nothing more than to marry the women who had claimed their hearts. Falcon found it not just hard but virtually impossible to imagine that *he* would ever fall in love—even though he accepted that it was his duty to marry and sire an heir…

MILLS & BOON PUBLISH EIGHT LARGE PRINT TITLES A MONTH. THESE ARE THE EIGHT TITLES FOR SEPTEMBER 2009.

❧

THE SICILIAN BOSS'S MISTRESS
Penny Jordan

PREGNANT WITH THE BILLIONAIRE'S BABY
Carole Mortimer

THE VENADICCI MARRIAGE VENGEANCE
Melanie Milburne

THE RUTHLESS BILLIONAIRE'S VIRGIN
Susan Stephens

ITALIAN TYCOON, SECRET SON
Lucy Gordon

ADOPTED: FAMILY IN A MILLION
Barbara McMahon

THE BILLIONAIRE'S BABY
Nicola Marsh

BLIND-DATE BABY
Fiona Harper

MILLS & BOON PUBLISH EIGHT LARGE PRINT TITLES A MONTH. THESE ARE THE EIGHT TITLES FOR OCTOBER 2009.

THE BILLIONAIRE'S BRIDE OF CONVENIENCE
Miranda Lee

VALENTINO'S LOVE-CHILD
Lucy Monroe

RUTHLESS AWAKENING
Sara Craven

THE ITALIAN COUNT'S DEFIANT BRIDE
Catherine George

OUTBACK HEIRESS, SURPRISE PROPOSAL
Margaret Way

HONEYMOON WITH THE BOSS
Jessica Hart

HIS PRINCESS IN THE MAKING
Melissa James

DREAM DATE WITH THE MILLIONAIRE
Melissa McClone

millsandboon.co.uk Community

Join Us!

The Community is the perfect place to meet and chat to kindred spirits who love books and reading as much as you do, but it's also the place to:

- **Get the inside scoop from authors about their latest books**
- **Learn how to write a romance book with advice from our editors**
- **Help us to continue publishing the best in women's fiction**
- **Share your thoughts on the books we publish**
- **Befriend other users**

Forums: Interact with each other as well as authors, editors and a whole host of other users worldwide.

Blogs: Every registered community member has their own blog to tell the world what they're up to and what's on their mind.

Book Challenge: We're aiming to read 5,000 books and have joined forces with The Reading Agency in our inaugural Book Challenge.

Profile Page: Showcase yourself and keep a record of your recent community activity.

Social Networking: We've added buttons at the end of every post to share via digg, Facebook, Google, Yahoo, technorati and de.licio.us.

www.millsandboon.co.uk